Mexico Is Missing

- AND OTHER STORIES -

J. David Stevens

THE OHIO STATE UNIVERSITY PRESS • *Columbus*

Copyright © 2006 by The Ohio State University Press.
All rights reserved.

Library of Congress Cataloging-in-Publication Data

Stevens, J. David, 1969–
  Mexico is missing and other stories / J. David Stevens.
     p. cm.
  ISBN 0-8142-5153-6 (pbk. : alk. paper) — ISBN 0-8142-9104-X (cd-rom)
  I. Title.
  PS3619.T4797M49 2006
  813'.6-dc22
                              2005028819

Cover design by Dan O'Dair.
Type set in Palatino by Jennifer Shoffey Forsythe.
Printed by McNaughton Gunn, Inc.

The paper used in this publication meets the minimum requirements of the
American National Standard for Information Sciences—Permanence of Paper
for Printed Library Materials. ANSI Z39.48–1992.

9 8 7 6 5 4 3 2 1

Contents

Contents

Acknowledgments

I am grateful for permission to reprint those stories that have appeared previously in the following magazines:

"To the Poet's Wife" and "The Mask," *Carolina Quarterly*
"The Hand Rebels," *Gulf Coast*
"What We Sell in the Room Today," *Notre Dame Review*
"Flying," *The Iowa Review*
"Great Myths of Our Time," *Many Mountains Moving*
"Mexico Is Missing," "The Postman," "Burn," "The Joke," "The President's Penis," and "Some Notes on the War," *Mid-American Reviews*
"The Suicide" and "Fish Story," *New Letters*
"My Mother's Lover" and "The Death of the Short Story," *The North American Review*
"Hunger" and "Why I Married the Porn Star," *The Paris Review*
"When the President Prays," *Press*
"Spelling Lessons," *Tampa Review*
"Clara's PC and the Second Coming," *The Virginia Quarterly Review*

To the Poet's Wife

You should not believe that poem about the plums. He didn't eat them so sweet and cold. I ate those plums, then wrote that note in his hand and laid two plum pits bright as marbles side by side on your table.

But he found that note before you did and took those pits and ground them into powder, then wet that powder to make ink. Then took that note—that sorry excuse for a note—and crossed it all through with plum pit to make lines. Then gave it to you and said it was a poem.

I watched through your window, plum juice staining my chin. I had three more plums in my pocket for later.

But I also had hope, because here I saw a woman who knew the value of plums over poems and wouldn't take a man's word over the genuine article any day of the week. You failed me, my dear. You ate those syllables, making the plums in my belly less sweet. And then you kissed him, which probably kept him going for days.

I couldn't eat after that. I left the plums by your wall near the sprinkler. Later, my friend who pushes the wheelbarrow saw three new plum trees in your yard. "That fruit grew *fast*," he said. "Looks sweet."

But I was off plums by then. "You want a sure bet," I told him, "stick with oranges."

I did not tell him about the dreams I was having: plum trees as far as one could see. I did not tell him how words ruin desire—how poems make men want both the thing itself and more than that thing, too.

In fact, I'm having trouble eating fruit at all: no guava or mango, no kiwi or elderberries. The fun has gone out of it, dear. And for what? What did I ever do to you? Me, harmless, a simple eater of plums.

Hunger

elen still had trouble believing her eyes: Walter, all five hundred pounds of him, lay naked in the bed with a girl, also naked, beneath him. Extending two fingers, Helen poked Walter's arm as if gauging the quality of a supermarket chicken. She asked the girl her name, and the muffled reply came back: *Genevieve.*

"'Are you sure he's dead?" Genevieve asked, tilting her head slightly to carry her voice past Walter's shoulder.

Helen poked Walter again, watching several rings of fat ripple around his bicep. "I've been married to him twenty-six years," she replied. "I think I can tell." She had no idea how long the girl had been this way, stranded beneath Walter, and was not sure she wanted to ask. In fact, she could only think how fortunate it was—if *fortunate* were the right word—that she had decided to take the train home for a few hours in the afternoon rather than stay through the evening in Manhattan. She was supposed to dine with the Glidden paint people at eight-thirty: *Oceana,* scallops, some shoptalk. She had not been able to get Walter on the phone earlier but had never imagined anything like this.

As Helen turned to leave the room, Genevieve muttered, "Are you calling the paramedics?"

"I have to cancel a meeting," Helen replied.

"Can't it wait?"

"I'm not sure. Are you in pain?"

"Well," the voice continued, "not really. A little warm."

"I'll turn down the AC," Helen replied, not sure what else to do.

She called her office—Walter was sick, she told her assistant—then came back with the portable phone. The room was cooler. Genevieve was moving what body parts she could. "Can you please put the blanket over my feet?" she asked Helen. "My toes are in the draft."

Out of reflex, Helen drifted down the two naked bodies and covered the girl's feet with the white cotton throw. For some reason, she was careful to loop the blanket around Walter's legs so that they remained exposed. As Genevieve's feet disappeared, Helen recalled that moment in *The Wizard of Oz* when the witch's legs curled inexplicably under the house and the ruby slippers appeared on Dorothy's feet. She saw the slippers clicking together in her head.

"That's much better, thank you," Genevieve said. There was a pause, as if each expected the other to do something.

Finally Helen put down the phone. "I'm going to push. When I get him far enough, you roll toward me." She leaned over Walter to where she could see the girl's face. Genevieve bumped her nose into Walter's meaty shoulder as she nodded. She had high cheekbones, brown hair, and dark brown eyes.

Against Helen's fists, Walter's belly seemed clammier and softer than usual. "Okay," she announced, then drove forward with all her might. She could not tell if Walter were moving or if she were merely sinking into him. Her stocking-feet skidded on the hardwood floor. "Anything?" she groaned.

"No, nothing."

Helen reached one leg back and propped it against the dresser. Then the other leg. Soon she was almost parallel to the floor, her legs driving the dresser into the wall against the full resistance of Walter's weight. Suspended in air, she marveled at how nimble her forty-eight-year-old body remained.

"Nothing," Genevieve repeated.

"Push with me, then."

"I'm pinned, you know? My arms. . . ."

Helen set her feet back on the floor. Part of her was tempted to leave, return to the ad agency for dinner, come back later to see what had shaken loose.

"I'm really sorry about this," Genevieve managed.

Helen frowned. "I'm going to move his legs. Maybe we can get him off a little at a time." She returned to the foot of the bed and wrapped both hands around one of Walter's ankles. Her fingers did not touch one another. She started to hoist his leg over Genevieve's.

"Ow. Ow! Stop!"

"What is it?"

"He's grinding into me. When you move his leg . . . I mean his hip . . . it falls right on me."

Helen realized what she was saying. Somehow, even in dying, Walter had managed to prop his body above the girl, using his arms and legs as supports. It was like some earthquake movie in which a man throws himself over the body of a child in order to protect it from a falling building. The problem—Helen realized—was that when she tugged on Walter's leg, that side of his body began to collapse. She would not be able to move Walter without having his entire weight, at least for a while, rest squarely on top of the girl.

For some reason, she remembered several times when she'd had to ask a man for help twisting the top off of a stubborn jar or bottle. She felt sick. She considered Walter's butt, pale and luminous, like a pile of snow melting in sunlight. "We'll have to call for help."

"The paramedics?"

Helen frowned. "I think we need more than that." She considered dialing 911 but decided that hers was not an emergency in the strictest sense. She checked the list of phone numbers in the bedstand, then dialed the Irvington fire department and explained the situation, then again. Finally the man at the other end said they would send a truck. Helen leaned over Walter to look Genevieve in the eye once more. "I'll wait downstairs."

"I wish you wouldn't. Talking makes me feel better."

"I'm not sure I want to talk."

There was a small cough. "I understand." Another cough.

Helen only felt more miserable. "Fine. I'll stay. But don't expect much." She crossed her arms and sucked in a whistling breath. Across Walter, she could see the Hudson River through the far window. A barge was moving slowly up the water's length toward the Tappan Zee. At night, Helen knew, the boat would have sounded its horn several times before reaching the bridge. She had often been wakened in darkness by the call of the barges—or else by Walter's snoring which, she only realized now, was about the same decibel-level. A small wake flipped outward from the barge's prow, the only visible sign that it was moving. She leaned against the dresser. "So, Genevieve, tell me about yourself."

"You can call me Gennie. I mean, my friends call me Gennie."

"All right," she acquiesced. "Gennie it is."

• • •

Walter and Helena had been living in Irvington for about nine years, ever since Walter had tired of Manhattan. He had weighed three-fifty back then and got out on a regular basis. It had only been a short skip from their three-room apartment across Central Park West to the park itself. Walter had always insisted on a regular afternoon stroll alone. "For my health," he had claimed. Once, purely by accident, Helen had spotted him on a bench near the Plaza with two bags of sugared peanuts.

Looking back, she found it amusing that Walter had been the one to insist on leaving the city. He had grown up in Glen Cove, and his father had done the daily Manhattan commute. Helen, by contrast, had grown up in western Virginia and met Walter during college in Richmond. She had loved to hear him talk about New York: SoHo, Jones Beach, Fifth Avenue, the Village. It had all sounded so exotic. They got the apartment across from the park right after they were married, with Walter's parents chipping in. Walter had gone to work for his father designing sports equipment. Helen had taken a position with a Midtown advertising firm. They had always talked about moving to the suburbs, whenever they had kids, but then they found out about Walter's sperm-count. They had taken it as a sign. They learned to live with things—and without—and stayed in New York.

So when Walter announced that he wanted to move out of the city, it took Helen by surprise. Even more surprising, he had quit his job without warning her. By then, Helen had started her own ad firm with three partners, so money was never an issue. She figured that Walter needed time to find himself. They bought a house the first day they went looking, a two-story white brick colonial in a suburb with wide streets, trees, and a park, just a half-block from the river. Walter kept gaining weight but seemed fine otherwise. After several months, he took a job doing sports reports for the local Westchester television station, becoming a small-time celebrity. He did man-about-town features from local bars and sometimes helped with the play-by-play for Army football. People began recognizing him whenever he and Helen went shopping in Scarsdale or White Plains. He seemed to like the attention.

Standing on her porch, Helen now noticed the way that the house's white bricks turned yellow, then red, with each revolution of the fire truck's lights. The head fireman, whose name was Sid, told her that he had not run the truck's siren out of respect for the delicacy of her problem. The lights, he insisted, were required by law.

"So," Sid began, "you're the wife?"

"What do you think?"

Sid was unfazed. "Just getting the facts, ma'am. Now this girl upstairs?"

"Gennie."

"Gennie, right. You don't know her or anything."

"Not until recently."

"But you see where I'm going? Who is she? Where'd she come from?" Sid paused at the door. "I need to rule out foul play."

Helen rolled her eyes. "She's a nineteen-year-old student at Pace. She met my husband last night watching the Mets at a sports bar."

Sid wavered, as if uncertain how to process the information. One of the other firemen stepped forward. "Against the Cardinals, chief. Leiter had a helluva game."

"Oh, yeah, the shutout."

"That's the one."

"I think they got a shot this year," Sid offered.

Helen wondered if they even believed her. "Would it hurt you to take this seriously?"

"Sorry, ma'am," Sid replied. "Emotional distance. It comes with the job."

They trooped upstairs, Helen in the lead, followed by Sid, Frank, and Louis. As they entered the bedroom, Helen turned just in time to see their smiles evaporate. "Holy crikes," Sid muttered.

For a few seconds they seemed stuck in the doorway, but then Sid inched toward the bed and bent tentatively over Walter's body. "How are you, Miss?" he said.

"Okay," Gennie replied. "Could you please help me here?"

Sid waved the other two men around the bed. He took hold of Walter's left shoulder, Frank grabbed the feet, and Louis took the right shoulder. "On three," Sid began. "One, two . . . *three!*" Walter's body jolted an inch upward then sunk back down. Sid looked at Louis, who shook his head. "We're going to need more leverage," Sid concluded. He put his knee onto the bed beside Walter. Frank came around the bed next to Sid and wrapped both arms under Walter's left leg. "Again!" Sid shouted.

As Walter popped up, there was a loud crack, and the bed beneath Sid and Frank plummeted several inches. The firemen hurried to ease Walter back down and climb off the mattress. Dropping to one knee, Louis peered under the bed. "The supports are breaking," he reported. "The whole thing could snap."

"Figures," Sid mumbled, looking at Helen as if this were somehow her fault.

Helen scrambled for something to say. "I guess you don't see stuff like this too often, huh."

"You'd be surprised," Sid told her. "You ever watch *Rescue 911?*" He bent down until the bed was at eye level. "He'll have to come straight up, I guess."

"We could brace him," Louis offered, "then knock the bed out from under him."

Sid shook his head. "Too risky. If it doesn't work, he falls onto the girl. And we don't have much room here. I don't even know how we'd get all the equipment upstairs—or how we'd get him down."

Gennie moaned. Frank stooped to console her then came up quickly. "Christ, that's Wassup Walter."

"Who?"

"You know, the Channel 12 sports guy. My kid's got a picture of him with Patrick Ewing."

"No shit?"

"No shit," said Frank. In his exuberance, he leaned back over Walter's head to look at Gennie. "You bagged yourself a celebrity, Miss."

"Shit, Frank," Louis exclaimed, motioning toward Helen.

"Oh, God . . . sorry, ma'am. I didn't mean anything."

Helen shrugged. "Why not? It's been one of those days." Everything was bothering her now, right down to the fact that the men kept calling Gennie *Miss* and her *Ma'am.* "If lifting him won't work, then what can you do?"

Sid was scanning the room. He looked at the ceiling then back at Walter. "Well, ma'am," he started, "how big are those skylights?"

Helen felt something inside her chest breaking. She looked up at the skylights, where the afternoon light had all but given way to dusk. She considered Louis and Frank, who were now staring at Walter like two boys examining their mother's lingerie drawer. "Look, you guys are going to keep this quiet, right? I mean, nobody else needs to be involved here."

Louis and Frank looked up. Everyone was still, and for a moment Helen could almost believe that Walter was not dead but merely awaiting an answer. Sid pushed out his chest, his face solemn. "Don't worry, ma'am," he said, as if that should settle it. "We're professionals." In the corner Louis nodded emphatically, while Frank made a zipping motion over his lips. Sid was looking at the skylights again. "Now if you could get me a pad and pen. I need to do a little math."

• • •

The first reporters arrived as Helen was descending the stairs to make some soup, mostly to give herself something to do. The van pulled right into the driveway, and two men started setting up lights along the sidewalk. The reporter, an attractive Asian woman, knocked on the door and, when Helen refused to answer, lifted the mail slot to call into the house. Finally Helen chained the door then opened it wide enough to deliver a hasty "No comment." As an afterthought, she told the news crew to get the hell off her lawn.

By nine o'clock, it was a small convention. Three news vans lined the street next to her Japanese maples, around whose trunks the police had strung a barrier of yellow tape. The neighbors were out, including several kids on bikes and skateboards, and the Hudson Diner had sent up some teenager to sell cappuccinos and biscotti from the back of his Honda. Helen cracked the shutter in a downstairs window and watched as her friends—Nell Constantine, Harry Silver, and Gabe Welsch—took turns in front of the cameras, motioning to the house.

She understood the impulse. In fact, she figured that TV would soon be a great help to her. She imagined herself making the talk-show rounds: *Oprah, Sally Jesse Raphael,* maybe even *Jerry Springer.* She could see the hosts now, speaking to her solicitously, compassion etched into their faces like the remnant of some disease. As she turned from the window, she let her gaze follow the residue of the camera-lights slipping through the room. There were colorful Chinese silk prints on three of the four walls—Walter's idea—with birds and fish and even a dragon. And on the fourth wall, beside the large bay window to the front yard, there was a picture of the gazebo at the University of Richmond where she and Walter had first kissed. Opposite the bay window slumped an off-white beast of a sofa, the only remnant of their apartment in New York with which Walter had refused to part. And in one corner was a huge oak armoire, whose faux front swung out in a single piece to reveal Walter's entertainment center: TV, VCR, video games.

It was a room with no continuity, Helen told herself, a room that people like her would keep only until the kids were grown and the pets were gone and there was no danger of nicer things being ruined. She and Walter had talked about getting a dog once. Helen had thought it would encourage him to get out and walk like he used to, but Walter had refused. "Can you imagine me responsible for someone else's life?" he'd asked. She had not pointed out the obvious then, that they were responsible for one another. But now, as she considered the TV cameras on her lawn, she chose to believe that he had known that. She chose to believe that *she* was the last thing to go through his mind before he died, like people who flash to clean underwear right before a car wreck. She pictured him in their bed, all five hundred pounds undulating in a wave, when he felt something inside his chest give out and said to himself, "Oh, crap, what will my wife think?"

His mother would have to be called, of course. And his brother in Red Bank. And an aunt whom Helen had met only once. The aunt lived in New Mexico but had been moving—Helen could not remember where. Florida maybe. And she would have to find a minister to do the service. And a good florist, too, nothing tacky. Thank God Walter had wanted to be cremated rather than buried. Helen wasn't sure they made coffins that big. She wasn't even sure, come to think of it, that they made crematorium furnaces that big. She suddenly thought of

Walter's remains, ashes and bits of bone fit into an urn that his mother would bury outside the family home on Long Island. The image surprised her: the ashes, the urn, Walter no bigger than other men.

There was a commotion outside. Returning to the window, she could see where one of the news spotlights had fallen into her geraniums. A police officer was reading the riot-act to two cameramen who were hoisting the equipment out of the flowerbed. She drifted into the kitchen, opened the refrigerator, but decided not to eat. An unopened can of Diet Coke sat just inside the door, so she pulled it out and headed upstairs. Earlier, she had covered both Gennie and Walter with a green sheet so that it looked like someone had pitched an army tent in the middle of her bed. She could tell that Gennie was trying to move as soon as she walked through the door. But, of course, the girl was going nowhere.

"You want a soda?" Helen asked.

There was a sigh. "I don't see why we have to wait like this."

"They can't run the crane in the dark. They need to see what they're doing."

"What if something goes wrong before morning?"

"There are police officers everywhere. And I told you that I set the phone to intercom. If you need anything, just yell."

"Still," Gennie continued, "it doesn't seem right."

Helen fished a Macy's flyer out of some old mail on the dresser, setting the cold drink on top of it. "Look, should I call someone? A friend? Your parents maybe?"

"Yeah, right. You tell me who would understand this?"

"I'm just trying to help," Helen answered, heading back toward the door.

"No, wait," Gennie continued. Walter's fat jiggled a bit as if the girl were waving her back. "Listen, I'm sorry. About all of this, I mean."

Helen moved to where she could see Gennie's forehead, the girl's brow rising and dropping with each word. "It's a little late for that," she said.

"If it means anything to you, this was the first time. I've never done anything like it before."

"It doesn't mean anything. I wish it did."

Gennie's brow wrinkled. "He was a nice guy."

"Excuse me?"

"Nice. You know, polite. He held the door for me, things like that."

"I don't need to hear this." She backed away.

"No, wait." Gennie cleared her throat. "I didn't mean it like that. Could you just wait a minute? Please?"

"And do what?"

"I don't know. Talk?"

Helen wanted to yell more than talk, even if part of her still felt sorry for this girl. She cleared her throat. "He was losing weight, you know." She hardly knew where the words were coming from. "He was serious about it this time."

There was a long pause before Gennie answered. "Most of the guys I date are on the thin side. Real beanpoles, actually."

Helen nodded. "He had an appointment with a doctor." At least he had said he did. One night, around the same time every year, Walter would knock back a few beers, get weepy, and promise Helen to drop some pounds. This year, he had gotten the name of a diet specialist from someone at the TV station. He had sat on the couch, half-drunk, waving the card in front of Helen's face and promising to call. In the dim bedroom, Helen decided to believe that he'd been telling the truth this time.

Gennie was rambling on. "If you had told me last week that this would happen, I'd have never believed it. I mean, he was a nice guy, but sleeping with him?"

For some reason, Helen was surprised to hear Walter's name used in the past tense. "Why did you?"

"Come again?"

"Sleep with him. Why did you?" She leaned over until she felt the heat of Gennie's breath rebounding off Walter's shoulder. The girl's eyes wavered, but there was nowhere for them to go.

"I don't know," Gennie admitted. "Just one of those things." Then as an afterthought, "I'd been drinking a little."

"Yeah," Helen replied.

"Well," Gennie went on, "why did you stay around? What kept you going?"

They stared at one another as Helen frowned, looking for an answer that should have been obvious. "It was a lot of things, I guess. We had a history." She backed away from the bed. "I have to go. Just yell if you need help." She could not tell if Gennie answered.

Downstairs again, she sank into the couch, the phone a few inches out of reach. She had Valium in the bathroom and considered taking a few pills, just to help her sleep, but then decided not to. She thought about Gennie. Partly she wished that she had stayed in the room and asked the girl to spill her guts—every last detail, the entire sordid affair. She closed her eyes and willed an image of Walter into her brain. What was the word that Gennie had used? Polite? She almost laughed at the thought of Walter in bed, a model of decorum, an elephantine Prince Charming cradling Cinderella's small calf in his hand. What kind of lover was that?

Still, she wanted to know. She remembered a conversation that she'd had with a cousin early in her marriage, when she and Walter were having problems and divorce was a real threat. Her cousin had asked, "How's the sex?" But Helen could not say. She had only been with two men, Walter included, and her first time—with her boyfriend's parents sleeping two rooms away—had been excruciating. She wanted to know for sure. It sounded insane, but part of her wanted to march back upstairs and ask point-blank, "Okay, how was he?"

Though maybe that question, she told herself, was just part of the larger question of how she and Walter had let things get so far. The year they'd had their problems, her job had forced her to do a lot of traveling. Walter was tipping three hundred then but had not lost all of the muscle that he'd had in college. There had been times on the road, Helen recalled, when she had imagined Walter turning up in the bar of her hotel unexpectedly. She would be in some unknown city—Chicago, Seattle, Dallas—and there he would be, looking as he had in college, when he did push-ups with her on his back and told her stories about all the foreign countries to which he had been.

Several headlights flashed by the window. The police were running off the crowds, though Helen knew they would return the next day. She laced her fingers across her stomach and noted the firm muscles beneath her blouse. She tried to remember what she'd had for lunch. Some lettuce with balsamic vinegar and a half-sandwich: turkey, maybe, or tuna salad.

It was strange, she thought, that death could make her forget what she'd had for lunch but remember things from years earlier—episodes she had dismissed that might have foreshadowed, if never quite explained, events in the present. Like the semester in college when she and Walter had written a paper together for a religion course, with the simple title "What Is Love?" They had been sitting together on the floor of Helen's dorm room, books and note cards strewn around them, when Helen decided to play a game in which they gave their own definitions, regardless of what the holy scholars said.

"Love is absolute," she began.

"Love is desperate," Walter shot back.

"Love is what keeps us going."

"Love doesn't admit failure, even when it should."

"Love," Helen said, "is the reward for life's hard work."

"Love," rejoined Walter, "is what we do because we can't bear anything else."

He went back to taking notes. Helen watched him a few more seconds, feeling something that was not quite disappointment inside her. She loved him. She was almost certain of it. Still, she made a mental note never to play that game again.

• • •

The midday sun reflected off the harness descending through the skylight. The firemen had arrived at dawn, but it had taken a while to move the news vans and onlookers back across the street, then to position the crane, then to have a contractor drive out to remove the skylight from its casement (this at Helen's suggestion, after Louis had come up the stairs with an axe). The crowd was smaller than the previous night, though Helen noted that many of her neighbors had taken the day off to watch, and the Hudson Diner kid was back with a sign that read "Bagel & Coffee $2.99." As the harness hit the bedroom floor, Sid spoke into his walkie-talkie. "Couple more feet. Okay, that's it. Hold it there." Outside, the crane's winching device fell silent. "All right," Sid continued, "let's get this puppy moving."

The three of them—Sid, Louis, and Frank—started unfolding the straps on the harness, then Sid unrolled a broad piece of canvas with the words "Property of Yonkers Raceway" emblazoned on one side. He caught Helen staring and quickly flipped the canvas so that the writing did not show. "We figured we would need something sturdier than our usual equipment," he explained.

One at a time, the firemen worked the straps as far up Walter's limbs as they could, cinching them tight. Walter's flesh seemed to ooze out of the restraints, pale white turning to dark red where the material constricted. "How are you, Miss?" Sid yelled.

"Okay," Gennie said. "Tired."

"It'll be over in a minute." Sid motioned toward Walter, "Now when I say go, the crane is going to lift him up a foot or two. We'll loop the canvas underneath him for more support. Then we'll take him straight up through the skylight. Louis, Frank, and me are going to guide him along, so I have to ask that everybody stay still until we get him out of the house. Understand?"

Gennie and Helen said that they did.

"Okay," Sid resumed, raising the walkie-talkie to his mouth. "Any last words?"

"I would appreciate," Helen said, "if you could keep him covered. I realize that it's silly to think about his dignity now, but. . . ."

Sid nodded. "We'll take care of it." He spoke a few words into the walkie-talkie, and there was the sound of a motor revving in the front yard. Slowly the slack in the line disappeared through the roof until the straps became taut around Walter's arms and legs. "Easy . . . easy," Sid said into the walkie-talkie.

Walter's belly shook, then there was a strange moment as he started to rise but his flesh seemed to flow back toward the bed. Louis and Frank leaned in from opposite sides of the mattress, keeping him steady and centering him beneath the skylight. Walter inched up a foot, another foot, until his knuckles were barely grazing the sheets.

"Stop," Sid commanded, and Walter jerked to a swaying halt in the middle of the bedroom. Quickly Louis threw the canvas under Walter to Frank, who wrapped it around Walter's middle and secured it to the clip at the end of the line. Then they took the green sheet and wove it between Walter's legs and around his waist a few times, tucking in the loose end at the small of his back. Helen could not help thinking that it looked like a giant green diaper.

"All right," Sid said, "Upsy daisy."

Walter resumed his ascent a few inches at a time, as if levitating. But his arms and legs drooped downward. Briefly Helen thought about how much weight he had endured. She began to understand, perhaps for the first time, just how bad living in his body must have been.

Before the skylight, Sid stopped the crane so that Frank and Louis could fit Walter squarely inside the casement's borders. Helen got her first look at Gennie and was surprised at how small, even emaciated, the girl seemed, especially in relation to her husband. Gennie rolled sideways to raise one leg so that only a small line of pubic hair was showing but otherwise made no attempt to cover herself. She lay there, staring upward, as Walter hovered over her.

Sid spoke into the walkie-talkie again, and Walter started through the casement. In the driveway, the reporters turned their cameras skyward. As Walter passed onto the roof, Helen moved to the foot of the bed so that she could look directly at him. She stood in his shadow, the sunlight filtering around him in a hazy corona, and imagined that he was reaching back for her—or for Gennie, or for both of them. When the crane shifted direction to take his body to the truck waiting in the road, his dangling hands swayed, as if simultaneously waving good-bye. She lifted her hand in response and suddenly felt the emotions tumble over her again—fear, longing, desperation, uncertainty, and in a small refracted place in the middle of these, love—until his shadow passed out of the skylight and she closed her eyes.

She waited until the firemen had left the room then sat down on the bed next to Gennie's feet. The girl seemed as stunned as ever. Helen considered her face, the thin lips, the eyes that were both sad and inviting. "He *was* a nice guy, wasn't he?" she managed.

"What?"

"Walter. He was a nice guy."

"Sure," Gennie's voice quavered. "The nicest."

That's how Helen wanted to remember him, the nice guy she married. She wanted to believe that she could. Again she thought about how large Walter had gotten, about how much hollowness there must have been in both of them. Desire and emptiness, she figured, with a thin line of mercy in the middle. It was a horrible way to live, but what was the alternative?

Behind her, Gennie was sitting up. Helen shifted to the head of the bed and carefully inserted a pillow behind the girl's back. The wind was blowing, and particles from the skylight spiraled to the floor. Gennie's tacky skin was thick with the scent of Walter's sweat. She had started to cry. "I swear to God," she whispered. "People are going to think I'm insane."

Helen thought about responding but instead moved one hand to Gennie's shoulder, feeling the slight chafe against her fingers as they stuck and unstuck on the girl's skin. She stayed this way until the paramedics came up, then stayed in the bedroom long after Gennie had gone. When her stomach growled, she made her way downstairs but turned into the living room, where she dropped onto the sofa, tucking her feet beneath her. The light from the afternoon sun made the room seem more garish than usual—the armoire, the silk prints—and Helen realized that even the sofa would have to go eventually. She had never understood Walter's desire to keep it; he'd only claimed to like it once the movers had gone to throw it out. She ran a hand over the seat. The off-white upholstery was pocked with stains, and the plush cushions attracted everything from loose change to crumbs to roving balls of dust. Perhaps someday, she thought, she would have an item custom-made: a divan covered in blue chintz or a maroon crushed-velvet chesterfield with golden tassels. She imagined them until she fell asleep—davenports and futons, chaise lounges and settees—each piece as fine as the next.

The Mask

He started wearing the mask because he lacked people skills. It was a plain mask—unpainted pine with slits for eyes and lips that turned neither up nor down. Wearing it in conversation, he would shout cues to make his feelings known. "I am smiling," he might say. Or, "I am frowning." People refused to look him directly in the face, but when the mask spoke, they could never wholly ignore it.

They started telling stories about the mask and decided that the man was the wisest among them, using as evidence the simple fact that he'd put on the mask to begin with. They made pilgrimages; they camped on the man's lawn. Not knowing what else to do, the man removed the mask during the night, setting it on his front stoop then sneaking out the back door. He assumed that, come morning, the people would see the mask and realize it was only a piece of wood.

But the people averted their eyes. They asked the mask questions and, when it did not answer, grew uneasy. Several bystanders were thrashed in the hope of appeasing it. Then, after the thrashing, the victims were carried to the front of the crowd to be miraculously healed.

Eventually a rainstorm soaked the mask. Termites got to it as well, gnawing it away in a week. The people took its disappearance as a sign. They began seeing its image in the world around them—in their dreams, their soup, the condensing steam from their showers. A local magistrate, who claimed to have been present for the mask's first appearance, began recounting what pleased it (meditation, good grades, bagels fresh from the oven) and what angered it (disobedience, inefficiency, navel rings). People in the audience tried to scribble down what was being said, but they couldn't hear exactly. They had bad seats. They filled in the details as best they could.

As for the man, he moved to a distant country, met a girl, came out of his shell—the usual story. Now and then he found himself wanting to talk about the mask, but his new friends might have gotten the wrong idea. They'd come to see him as a decorous man, possessing diplomatic skill, and he did not think it prudent to ruin that image over one unchangeable folly from his youth.

Mexico Is Missing

nd even though the tabloids ran the story first, everyone else was quick to hop on: NPR, the networks, CNN, until you had no choice but to believe—even if you didn't want to—that Mexico was missing, and I know they sent people down to investigate, because I got word from Johnson who has a friend, Richardson, at the *Times,* who was sent by his editors to find out if Mexico was indeed missing (even though Richardson had never been to Mexico, which made his editors say, good, you'll have an unbiased eye), but not knowing directions exactly, Richardson went to Tucson and asked the people there how to get to Mexico, and they said turn left, so Richardson did, and all he saw was the horizon, that big long red dirt Western horizon, which made it incredibly easy to believe that beyond was nothing, the end of the earth, and so Richardson said should I be able to see Mexico from here, and the Tucsonians all said it's tough to say, but would you like to come in for a lemonade because even though it's dry heat it's still one hundred and thirty degrees out here, so Richardson entered their homes for lemonade and decided who would it hurt to confirm the report (he had done everything within his power, after all) that Mexico was missing, and so the *Times* ran the story, and whenever one reads something like that in the *Times*—well, you see where I'm going—and it's not like anyone rushed to deny the report, not even the Canadians, with their quick affirmation of their own existence, or the State Department with its mixed report expressing regret but also noting how Mexico had had problems in the past, of which disappearance is sometimes a result, which was the angle that all the talk shows took, even weeks later when Jimmy Rex had on the geologist, the economist, the anthropologist, and the conservative politician, and the geologist talked about possible "silent" earthquakes, and the economist talked about downward sloping market trends, and the anthropologist brought up ancient Mayan myths, and the politician first said aliens but then said DRUGS, until Jimmy himself had to step in and say but, gentlemen, never before in history has anything caused a nation simply not to exist, which shut them all up for a second, until the geologist said yes that's right, and the anthropologist said you've hit the nail on the head Jimmy Rex, and the economist said that's why you're number one in the ratings Jimmy my boy, and the politician admitted later that Jimmy Rex was a formidable adversary, which is only to say that you couldn't get away from the story, even if you didn't want to believe that Mexico was missing, because it was everywhere, Belize calling for a UN probe, Guatemala casting dispersions on the CIA, Panama wondering if Mexico's disappearance would make the Canal obsolete, and jokes everywhere about the President's comment on not having good *carne asada* again, and private sources telling the media that what he really meant was Mexican women, which raised not only hue but also cry from the feminist groups, and then the jokes about the President not keeping his zipper up, even in foreign countries, but all of those jokes depending on this implicit acknowledgement—even at a conversational level—that Mexico was indeed gone gone gone, until it became too much to bear, watching the Mexicans in foreign countries lamenting how they would never see their homeland again, the Red Cross mobilizing for no apparent reason, and the actor-spokesmen, like Alex Bassinger and Ted Kitman, on screen asking for help with the relief effort until you felt guilty if you hadn't stacked canned goods and clothing and toys and your checkbook and the pink slip to your '65 Mustang by the door, patiently awaiting the relief workers who would come pick them up, but who would never really come because there was such an overwhelming outpouring of public support, and no one knew what to do with all the aid that had been offered, except for a con man or two, which should have made it easy to believe that Mexico was not in fact missing, except that they kept counting the days on C-SPAN with their Missing Mexico Watch and started running retrospectives in the magazines from famous people formerly associated with Mexico and even held an essay contest for grade-schoolers—Mexico, What It Meant To Me— not to mention the non-stop Westerns running on the cable stations, whose titles ran together, Don't Forget The Ruby River Way We Won The West When Santa Anna Was Here To Stop 'Em Boys With Six Bullets To A Gun, even though none of these really presented Mexicans in the most flattering light, except occasionally for a beautiful and fiery Mexican girl or an idealistic young soldier (who were usually both Anglo actors with a lot of face paint), but none of that seemed to bother Nielsen audiences because everyone was so starved for anything Mexican that it seemed to some people Mexico had never really left, what with all the Made-in-China Mexican items flooding the markets, and getting snapped up to the point that you couldn't even find a can of refried beans on the shelf at A&P, and small-business owners admitting in private that maybe it wasn't such a bad thing about Mexico disappearing, what with the potential for merchandising and the stock market turning bullish and the S&P index looking good and the Fed surprisingly not raising the interest rates, all of which caused such an overall surge that even market analysts, the brave ones at any rate, were willing to suggest—though only suggest mind you—Mexico's central fiscal role, as if the disappearance had been guided by some transcendental free-market hand and things could not have worked out better if we had planned them, and even if you were a little suspicious of such coincidence you had cash in your pocket, assuming you had invested wisely, and a little cash always helps smooth over doubt, which is probably why nobody followed up on reports of the people appearing at the border from that place where Mexico had been, calling themselves Mexican, and showing the border guards things that seemed Mexican enough (an Aztec fertility idol, the green and purple flower of a rare cactus, a blue-painted burro named Los Angeles Ed) and saying in Spanish as well as in English and in other languages that Mexico was not missing, it was where it had always been, but the guards refusing to look because they had heard on TV that, where Mexico once was, there now existed a giant mist capable of stealing a man's soul, which sounded so ludicrous that the crowd of people staged a sit-down strike to force the guards to take a peek, and drank coffee until they had to pee very badly, and watched a Johnny Hopper show about women who love women who once were men having affairs with their mothers (and the people said to each other, "They call *us* backwards . . .") after which came several hours of news in which Mexico's disappearance was again discussed, and you could see it on their faces that, while they didn't believe the reports, they were beginning to see how other people could be swayed by such coverage, and they did have to pee very badly, and it was getting toward the dinner hour, and someone in back said it'll blow over soon enough, and several others nodded in a way that was no longer angry and certainly not defeated, but accepting in a way that people often resort to when confronted by items which—however false—have such a convincing aspect of truth that they are hard to deny, a look that combines disappointment with a touch of understanding and maybe even a touch of fear about losing sight of the truth themselves, such that while some of the people vowed to stay until the guards agreed to turn their heads, most said it's not really worth it, is it, when you have the truth on your side, just let the facts come out, because people who don't want to believe these lies eventually won't, even though it was obvious how difficult it was for them to concede that word *eventually,* wanting so much for the news to come out *immediately,* the kind of desire which as one small woman noted was probably what got everyone into this mess to begin with, but by then the people were balling up their coffee cups and telling their few friends who stayed that they would bring leftovers later (and she was a *very* small woman with a *very* soft voice) and someone else in the crowd was grumbling about how it was time to fight fight fight, but how do you fight words, which was all that was really left to them as they shrugged in frustration and clapped their hands to each other's shoulders, the frightened guards still refusing to look as the crowd collectively wheeled southward and seemed to fall into its own long shadow as it began the slow plod home

What We Sell
in the Room Today

I n the room today we sell only this thing, not that. If you want that thing, you must select another room. Each room sells its own thing and nothing else. If you need directions to other rooms, we will grudgingly provide a map.

We can sell this thing however you like. In a plain brown wrapper. In a shiny blue box. Around the neck of a German named Helga—or Heinrich, your choice. We do not ask questions unless you request them.

We offer delivery, though it costs. Extra too is personal service. You must pay to be called by your own name or pay to be called by another. And it's extra should you begin with your own name then switch to an alias like "Naughty Puppy" or "Jesus Christ." Of course, only one name per credit card.

Talking is permitted but discouraged; the spoken word is messy and imprecise. Instead we ask that you print your order on the notepads provided and slide it through the slot by the door for processing. We do not handle complaints. If you are not satisfied, fill out another order. Be specific, then patient. Remember that everyone else is ordering, too.

Please know that your anonymity is guaranteed. When billing, we list ourselves as "Technical Support." We do not consider this a complete lie.

We will answer some questions but not others. Questions we will answer include *How much? How fast?* and *How often?* Questions we will not answer include *Why?*

Care is a separate issue. We can provide it for a price but do not guarantee authenticity. Benevolence and generosity are out of the question, though mercy is available on a seasonal basis. It can be found in another room not specified on the map.

This offer is for a limited time and subject to change without notice. Don't miss out on the savings. Remember that you are a valuable customer and, of course, that you will buy eventually. And if the other rooms should look exactly like this one, don't be alarmed. Direct your questions through the slot by the door, then dutifully await your answer. A representative will be with you shortly.

The Postman

T he Postman carries two satchels: one empty and one full. "For worthwhile ideas," he tells me as he shakes the empty bag. I ask him if he has ever found anything to fill it. He stares at me as if somehow betrayed.

• • •

The Postman is not a tall man, but he is not short either. You would not pick him out of a Postman crowd. Still, the word *average* fails to describe him. He switches outfits often, and though I have watched for several months I have never seen him repeat an ensemble exactly. He always makes some change: red scarf with orange Bermudas, mauve scarf with blue knickers, a sequined garter worn just over the knee. Once he appeared at my door with writing across his knuckles. "Each day is different," his right hand read. And on his left, "Learn to accessorize."

• • •

On Thursday I receive a letter from my Aunt Louise, the gas bill, a pre-approved credit card, and a sweepstakes entry-form bearing someone else's name. The Postman hands the envelopes to me one by one. "The fault lies not in the stars," he says, "but in over-priced sodas, Rottweilers, and uncomfortable shoes." Aunt Louise, I discover later, merely wants to tell me that she's doing okay.

• • •

There are twelve mailboxes on our street, arranged in perfect symmetry thus:

1	2	3	4	5	6
7	8	9	10	11	12

I am number 7, like the lucky roll in dice. "Or like the sins," the Postman observes. A superstitious man, he refuses to visit the houses in order but has a different routine for each day. To figure the Postman out, I track his daily movements then record them in a notebook. I draw a line from house to house to indicate the route he takes. Saturday evenings I review my findings, seeking a pattern; each new addition looks like violin strings played by a bear. Undaunted, I tape the drawings to the ceiling fan then watch them spin at various speeds, searching like an ancient shaman for answers from above.

• • •

"There are basically two kinds of people," the Postman says, "those who are satisfied with empty satchels and those who are trying to fill them." I ask the Postman how long it takes to fill a satchel on average. He frowns, "That is hardly the point."

• • •

Friday brings the water bill, a copy of *Scientific American,* and a picture-postcard of my insurance agent standing next to a reclining Buddha in Thailand. He writes that he has enjoyed his travels in Asia then asks me to consider an umbrella policy. The Postman slaps a bee to the ground, stomping it dead. "Chaos is beautiful," he observes, "but so damn untidy."

• • •

Sometimes I watch the Postman from the room upstairs. Like everyone, he has good days and bad and, during the bad ones, is given to passionate outbursts at the sky. In the street, he extends his arms in a vaguely religious pose and screams, "Where are those souls I used to love?" then waits silently as if expecting an answer. Sometimes he lifts his full satchel above his head like a sacrifice. Sometimes he sits Indian-style on the asphalt and devours old Ms. Whimpole's Dessert-of-the-Month Club selection.

• • •

Saturday I get nothing. The Postman hides at the corner of the house, observing my reaction.

• • •

The Postman perceives my desire to understand the links between us. In return, he acts genuinely concerned about the mail I receive. "Is it what you expected?" he asks, passing me an envelope. "Is it what you want?" Once I received a letter from a woman I had loved, who told me that she'd always despised me and that her therapist had instructed her to get her issues into the open. She did not leave a return address. "Do you derive pleasure from unexpected events?" the Postman wondered. "Or do you fear the inevitable: junk mail, solicitations, anything labeled IRS?"

• • •

Sundays I leave my trash by the curb for collection. Though I can't be sure, I believe the Postman picks through my garbage, inspecting what mail-items I have and have not thrown out. Occasionally he retrieves one and, feigning ignorance, delivers it to me again during the week: a flier for a Veterans' Association, an ad for the local symphony, a lingerie catalogue pocked in one corner by fried-chicken grease. When I suggest they are items I have seen before, the Postman turns pensive, shuffling his feet. "I am not a source but a conduit," he claims. "Not the great idea but the hand writing it down."

• • •

Now and then the Postman is assisted by Postal Trainees, smartly dressed men in blue and red, marching up the street in tight formation like ducklings or the Chinese army. Stationed one to each house, the trainees wait until the Postman blows his whistle, then they hup-hup to their respective doors, deliver the mail, and resume their formation in the street. The Postman motions toward them, smiling. "And the song goes on," he observes. When I ask if I can blow the whistle, he says that I am not ready. "Maybe next time," he muses.

• • •

I cannot lie to myself, of course. I know that the Postman is insane and that I am insane for watching him. Still, something draws me to his routine. I cannot begin my day until he has come and gone, and I find myself sleeping later and later, just so that I don't have to wait too long for him once out of bed. On days when he is late, I am inconsolable. On days when he brings no letters, I am lost. The Postman knows this. He waits at the top of the hill and watches as I pull aside blinds, open shutters, crack doors. He jogs past the house.

• • •

Monday brings me copies of *GQ, Fortune,* and *Sexy Singles.* "Oh, our desire for acceptance," the Postman laments, "what to wear, what to want, who to love. Can't you see what you need simply by opening your eyes?" His conviction seems so profound that I decide not to point out how none of the names on the magazines are mine.

• • •

Once a telephone lineman was beaten up and thrown in a dipsy-dumpster down the block. He claimed not to have seen his assailant, who attacked from behind. The only lead the police had to pursue was the quote *What hath God wrought?* which the attacker chanted repeatedly while slicing the line on which the phone man had been working. Later, having my suspicions, I asked the Postman his opinion on the attacker's motives. After a long moment, the Postman replied, "Only arrogant fools presume to discover why."

• • •

In my notebook I scribble down all that the Postman does in an attempt to learn his secrets. The observations take shape in a chain linking page to page. The Postman steps in gum—the Postman adjusts his crotch—the Postman scrapes the gum on the Hathaways' walk then delivers their mail—the Postman whistles (what does he whistle?)—the Postman digs in his right ear with his pinky finger—the Postman barks at the O'Connells' mutt—the Postman looks toward my house (does he see me? does he care?)—the Postman delivers my mail—the Postman tells me that we are greater and lesser than the universe intended us to be—the Postman twirls his empty satchel like a matador's cape—the Postman stares directly at me—he says, "Hey, what are you writing there?"

• • •

Tuesday I receive a pack of underwear from Aunt Louise and a flier from a car dealership telling me not to be fooled by other offers. "Truth," the Postman snorts. "You only know that I bring the mail. Everything else is negotiable."

• • •

I have a feeling that I would be all right if I could only get the Postman out of my head. Frankly there are days when I would throttle him for a penny, leaping through the screen-door, watching his expression turn from surprise to a kind of acceptance as my hands tighten around his throat. We would lie on the front lawn, amid the electricity bills and music club brochures, like irreconcilable lovers. And as the Postman opened his mouth to make whatever final confession he might make to me, I would say over and over, "I don't want to know."

• • •

The Postman once brought a package wrapped in stiff brown paper. Inside was a cardboard box, holding another box, holding another box, until there were ten boxes total. The Postman noted my perplexed expression. "It's not the boxes that are important," he told me. "It's the fact that they reached you at all."

• • •

Wednesday I receive a post card from a Pentecostal Church asking if I've been saved. In the distance the Postman slumps under the weight of his satchels, like a man carrying water through the desert. I try not to think of him as a prophet but only a man, for all his machinations, who will eventually die of thirst.

• • •

Why did the Postman cross the road? Which came first: the Postman or the letter? How come packages take as long to cross town as they do to cross the country? "These questions comprise the single mystery," the Postman claims. "All other mysteries flow from them."

• • •

Sometimes, waking unexpectedly, I stare from my bedroom window and wonder where the Postman is or what he is thinking. Usually such nights are clear ones. The moon rises over the town and splits the night, stealing some of the darkness's power. I know that the darkness has no power really. Light comes and goes in a cycle governed by inertia, centripetal force, and gravitational pull. Tomorrow the Postman will deliver my mail at the normal time, slave to the same cycle. Nonetheless, I continue to watch and wait. I imagine that I will one day find an empty satchel slung over my mailbox with a note attached that reads, "Use it well." The neighborhood will be still. Noise, if there is any, will be indistinct and distant. I will raise my fingers and imagine that I can feel a kind of steady wind, letters like invisible petals flung onto the air, circling the earth, waiting to be read. Meanwhile the Postman will be watching in secret from the top of the hill. He will nod to himself not so much out of knowledge but out of a sense of the inevitable, like conversation passed between people who fear one another but who fear silence even more. The air will be comfortably chilly. Deer will edge from the woods to sniff the air. Sleeping dogs will dream happily, passing gas as their back legs tremble. And for reasons that only he can fathom, the Postman will be smiling.

Flying

immy names one piglet Wilbur and the other Orville, then sets about making them fly. It is two years before the war's beginning, when Jimmy is fifteen, and I am nine.

My job is to watch the pigs and make sure they don't eat too much. Also I'm supposed to bring Jimmy supplies when he asks. We've been storing them in the barn: an old boat sail, some copper pipe, three discarded leather harnesses, a pile of empty potato sacks.

"You know what this means," Jimmy asks, "when pigs fly? It's like guaranteeing your dreams will come true. No more taxes for Mom and Dad. You'll get that Huffy bike you want. And Karen Egerton will finally go out with me." He holds a couple of screws between his teeth, then takes them out to say, "Maybe up to the reservoir."

And then we are ready. In the middle of the south field, already cut, we slide Orville and Wilbur's legs through the holes we've made in the sacks, then tug on the harness lines to make sure they're secured to the frame. Jimmy wheels out the motorcycle that Dad brought back after Korea, ties the two lead ropes under the seat, then starts slowly forward. Orville and Wilbur jump up several feet, bump the ground, squeal, then jump up again, skimming the grass. As Jimmy accelerates, they rise higher into the air—like a kite, like a hawk with a pair of stones in its grip. Jimmy makes a broad circle to keep his speed steady, while I chase behind them, laughing and thinking about the Huffy bike that will soon be mine.

It's hard to believe that four years from now Orville, big as a freezer, will win first prize at the county fair. I'll ship the blue ribbon to Jimmy in Vietnam but never know if he gets it, since it will not come back to us in the packet of belongings the army sends.

For the moment, though, Vietnam is not a name I recognize. Instead, I feel my breath grow short from running, and I stop and wave both arms as if to confirm that I'm still there. Jimmy makes a loop at the far end of the field, and as he turns I can see that he is smiling, proud. In the distance, they seem more firmly connected than they are: my brother and these two pigs. All of us seem connected actually, all of us still children, time and innocence and possibility, until the wind unexpectedly shifts, and the pigs drift irrevocably to ground.

JFK's Shoes

don't know why I told Delia about JFK's shoes. Looking back, I realize she might not have been the woman I thought. I loved her, sure. But some secrets can't stay afloat between two people, not even with love buoying them up.

On the card table between us, the shoes looked downright ordinary: black dress lace-ups, though a cut above the ones I bought at Payless to match my church suit. The first time Clue had shown them to me, I'd expected bigger, or maybe smaller. Something special at any rate. But there they were as they had been every year of my life, hopelessly normal.

Delia craned her neck to look down the sides. I could tell she wanted to touch them. "Give me the story again," she said.

"Clue worked at Parkland Memorial," I repeated. Then, because she seemed to want more, "He was an orderly. People trusted him."

She brought her face in real close to the tips. It made me uncomfortable the way she was staring. I mean, I understood the bomb I'd dropped on her, but these were the shoes, after all. *The* shoes. They deserved some respect. Clue had always tried to sound like a doctor when he considered them. "Them spatters on the toe," he'd said the first time he showed me, "I reckon that's blood. And that there," he continued, pointing to what looked like a crumb of dried sponge caught where the leather creased beneath the laces, "that might've come straight out his brain. Can you imagine?"

Delia had never met Clue, and there was something about him she didn't trust. "If you were normal people, you'd have called him Grandpa. How did he get that nickname anyway?" She drew the word out like it was three parts instead of one: *Cl-u-ue.*

I never had a good answer for her. Even before she told me, I must've known my family was shakier than most, but everybody's messed up somehow. I figured, why dwell?

Delia couldn't stand that logic. She was a "make your own bed and lie in it" sort. She'd done a two-year Associate's Degree at a community college in Wilmington, North Carolina, then moved to Richmond after sleeping with a West End realtor she'd met at a bar in Nags Head. He'd kept her four months in an apartment off West Broad, promising marriage, until she saw him at Regency Square with his real wife and daughter. She went to his house later on. I never got the whole story, but she did tell me that their final conversation involved a weed whacker, two bottles of Karo syrup, and his BMW 3-series. Delia is not a woman to be trifled with.

She stayed in Richmond, though, and took a paralegal job with Bill Trufield, the TV lawyer with commercials about being hurt through the fault of others. I guess I should have been grateful to him because, without that job, Delia would have been long gone, but there was just something off-nut about him. He was as fat as the end of an opera and about as slick as razor stubble, though in his own mind he was the whole tub of Crisco. His face turned red whenever he thought for more than a second, like there was too much blood circling his brain. Still, Delia said he had the only two qualities in a male boss that she cared about. He paid her on time, and he knew where to keep his hands.

He'd just given her a raise, in fact, and it was the money that started us down the road to JFK's shoes. That night after dinner, she'd announced it was time to get long-term serious. She said that the raise made her a woman with prospects. And there I was working at the Reynolds Metals plant like always. I needed to get religion, she told me, or at least a dental plan. "Seems to me," she declared, "that two people headed for the blessed land of matrimony should have something of true value to rub between them. Don't you think?"

She made marriage sound like a town in western Georgia. "My love is true value," I told her. "And you'll never have to worry for something to rub between us."

But it was the wrong time to joke. Delia can act real put-upon when she wants. One of her grandmas was Irish, so she thinks she's got a lock on pain. "If funny were grapes," she said, "you'd drink your wine from a thimble."

"There's always whiskey."

"Don't start." She frowned. "You're two full years younger than me, and you got no idea what it means. I'm hearing clocks everywhere." Truth is, she was a sexy thirty-six, thin and tan and brown-haired that turned almost blond in the summers. If she hadn't reminded me on a regular basis, I could've forgotten how old she really was. Even the guy at the ABC store carded her every other time she went in. But it was no use when she started hearing clocks. That sound shut down everything else completely. "My life has been no cake-walk," she continued, "and I deserve certain things before succumbing to middle age."

She had all the drama of a heart attack at a hanging. Inside, I cursed that West End realtor who'd turned her up in knots. But even I knew it was more than that. Delia liked to tell the story about her no-account brother, Roger, who'd won ten thousand dollars during the "Chuck-for-Bucks" contest at the halftime of a Tennessee football game. To me, old Rog just showed that the world turned how it wanted and didn't give a jig for us. But to Delia he proved something else: that everybody's luck came due eventually. And given how much better a person she was than Roger, she imagined her payoff would be a truckload.

So I showed her the shoes.

My point was just to let her know that we were all right, I guess, that there was something connecting us to God and everybody, and maybe when you have a thing like that, ten thousand dollars doesn't seem so much. It was working, too. I could tell she was happy. She pulled back from the shoes and said, "I'll be dogged." Then she leaned back in and kind of sniffed them, then turned to smile at me like I'd just found a necklace she'd lost as a girl. "I'll be dogged," she said again.

It wasn't until later, after I'd slipped the shoes back into their paper Ukrops bag and tucked the bag under several old blankets in my closet, that I caught Delia on eBay at the computer in our bedroom. "There's nothing like them," she reported.

"Nothing like what?"

"The shoes, Jakey. What else?"

I always had to worry when she called me Jakey. "Deel," I said, "you're not trying to sell them, are you?"

"I'm just fixing their value, is all."

"Their value," I told her, "can't be touched by cash."

The wind went out of her cheeks a little, but she recovered quickly. "I'm not talking heirloom value," she said. "Face it, Jake, your stuff is only worth what someone else will give you for it."

"But why do we need to know?"

"It's just prudent. More knowledge beats less." She turned off the computer screen and moved to the bed, curling up a little on her side and patting the cover. "Don't worry," she said. "I'd never do anything without asking you first."

She started unbuttoning her blouse. I knew what she was up to, but I let her do it anyway. I am not the kind of man to force relations when they're not wanted, but I won't turn down a free lunch either. And it was good sex. Delia was trying to pump the well of my stubbornness, so she went at things with purpose. She almost made me forget, too. Only afterward, when she fell asleep, did her lips curl into that smile again, and every one of her little snores was a word pressed into my restless ears: *shoes shoes shoes shoes.*

• • •

It wasn't like my life had been so great. My mother died when I was four. By then, she'd been three years out of the house, having left me in the playpen with a note for my father to find after work. I can't say that I knew her. We never spoke, not once, unless it was those words she whispered to me in that first year of my life, that I hear in my dreams sometimes and wonder if I'm remembering. She was half-Welsh, half-Puerto Rican, a short circuit waiting to happen. She'd been killed by a New York City bus, stepping off the wrong curb in Astoria, Queens. For years after, my friends avoided talk about any public transportation, in particular the chance of death thereby.

My mother had met Dad in Fayetteville, North Carolina, where he was training at Fort Bragg. She'd followed another man down from New Jersey on the promise of marriage, but he'd lost the ring-money in a poker game his third night on base. Dad found her in a bar. From the few pictures he kept, I know that she was a special beauty, thin with dark hair from her Puerto Rican side, but light green eyes and skin like raw cotton from the Welsh. Dad was no slouch either, and there's that line about a man in uniform. Maybe he should have known better, given the circumstances, but he was still at a point where he could dream. I was born six months after they married.

Dad had joined up right out of high school, hoping to jump out of planes and kill communists with nothing but his pinky finger. When he fainted during airborne training, though, he woke up to the writing on the obstacle course wall. They shipped him off to the kitchen, where he figured he would do his four years and out. But there he discovered an unexpected talent for quiche. The army gave him special training. He cooked for the officers, then eventually moved to Fort Lee in Petersburg with a new set of stripes, where he trained other kids to cook for the officers. Sergeant Sauté, they called him behind his back, but I think he liked it. Thirty-six years, and he still toed the good soldier line. "We're each called to duty in our own way," he'd say, whenever anyone asked why he joined in the first place.

Clue had been the wild card in all this, my father's father—"In sperm only," Dad liked to say. He had come up through the Great Depression, an orphan, and served a four-year navy hitch in the South Pacific during World War II, though the closest he ever got to any Japanese was a bottle of sake that he stole from a shipmate on a three-day pass in Sydney. He didn't even know he had a son until he got back to San Francisco in 1945. He said that he never got the letters, though chances were good that he just hadn't read them, and my grandmother was just a girl who'd once showed a sailor some kindness as he headed off to certain death. By the time Clue put things together, my father was already three, living with my grandmother and her parents in Spokane. Clue tracked them down, to his credit, but the two-hour conference on that porch in Washington was anything but pleasant. He promised to return when he was a man fit to marry a decent girl, which was the nicest goodbye he could figure. He bounced in and out of my father's life from then on, without warning or reason.

But part of him must have liked being a daddy, because he never disappeared outright.

He told me once that he had seen me in the hospital after I was born, but I can't imagine how. The first time I remember seeing him, I was seven years old and just home from school, standing in the front yard of our house in Colonial Heights. He came roaring up the driveway in a pickup with Ohio plates, spinning gravel before he stopped, then hopped out and stalked across what passed for our lawn, hoisted me up, and said, "Hell yes, Jacob, give grampy a kiss." A girl got out of the passenger side, maybe a third his age, wearing a Rolling Stones tank top and carrying a knapsack covered with buttons that claimed she smoked pot for breakfast. She called his name, and he put me down, then they went inside and screwed the rest of the afternoon—the guest room bed banging against the wall—while I watched cartoons on the black-and-white in the kitchen. I had no idea who he was. Later, when Dad got home, Clue bought chicken from Golden Skillet, which we ate off paper towels, while the girl, Sally, told us about her plans to start a commune in Mexico where they'd grow some of the highest-grade weed in the world and maybe vegetables, to give to lepers and whatnot. Clue had promised to take her as far as Missouri. By the next morning, they were gone.

He showed up this way about once a year, sometimes for a night, sometimes more. The longest he ever stayed was two full weeks when I was eight, in a mustard RV in the driveway. That time he came with a woman named Rosalinda, about his age, who washed my clothes and every morning made me eggs with salsa on them. I still remember it as two of the best weeks of my life.

The RV was jammed with the crap of Clue's travels: a WWI bayonet with which he pulled pineapple slices out of cans, a yellow traffic sign that read "Elk Crossing," posters advertising three months' worth of Grateful Dead concerts. He had a collection of fifty license plates, one for every car he'd driven in every state in the country. He showed them to me, starting with Alabama and working through alphabetically, until he reached Texas. That's when he remembered the shoes.

He kept them in a plain box, though he'd tied it carefully with two brown hair ribbons and put it on its own shelf for safekeeping. I didn't know who Kennedy was, but Clue filled in the gaps. "Jacob, I've stolen lots of things in my time," he said, and I thought how funny it was that he always called me by my right name, Jacob, even though he didn't stand on ceremony anywhere else. "I wouldn't recommend it as a lifestyle," he continued, "but sometimes good results come in back-ass ways." He showed me the shoes every visit after that, and he made sure I understood that they were to be protected above all his other things—that I was to watch out for them when he was gone. "It ain't much," he told me, "but at day's end, all we've got is the history we write."

Dad and I only knew he'd died when the RV showed up in our driveway again. I was fourteen. I answered the bell to this freezer-sized black man, who told me that he had instructions to bring the RV to our address. He didn't ask me to sign anything but turned around and walked back up the street as if he lived one block over. By the time Dad got home, I'd been in the camper for hours. I was playing this game with the bayonet where I tried to see how many times I could flip it in the air and still catch it on the non-blade end. Dad asked about Clue, and after I explained, he told me not to touch anything.

"Why not?" I asked him.

"Because."

And it became suddenly clear to me that Clue's death had freed him up. The man he'd tolerated in life was no longer around to demand that tolerance. It was a weird feeling for me, I guess, and sad. That night, while Dad slept, I snuck out to the RV and got JFK's shoes off the shelf, then hid them as far back in my closet as they'd go. When I returned from school two days later, the RV was gone, and Dad and I never talked about Clue again.

• • •

Delia took a few weeks to make her move. She'd been cooking more, soda bread and corn pudding and pork roasts straight from the Crock Pot where the meat just fell off the bone. It was a Saturday, and I was coming back from the softball fields—warm beer, and we'd had to forfeit our second game because Joe Bemis needed to pick up his wife from her Tantric Yoga class. Delia had the shoes on the card table set up in the living room. There were little triangles of Wonder bread with pimento cheese and plastic plates, the good ones, whose dark green color always reminded me of the dresses that girls wore to church at Christmas. "Hey, Jakey," Delia said when she saw me. Bill Trufield, his eyes even with the table, hoisted himself up like a water buffalo coming out of the drink.

"Jake," he said, smiling like a friend.

I motioned to the table. "What've we got here?"

Delia looked at Bill, who spread his hands. "Delia told me your story, and I agreed to make a few inquiries. I think I have some news."

They waited as I pushed a pimento sandwich into the corner of my mouth, then dropped into a chair, trying to look unconcerned. My coming home early had rattled them both, but their natural sense of drama kicked right back in. When they continued, I felt like a test audience for the Home Shopping Network.

"Now like I was saying," Bill resumed, "they've been excellently kept." He leaned forward and swished one hand around them, some evil-universe version of Vanna White. His pale fingers resembled partly melted candles, bent into sections but still hanging on at the wick.

"Didn't I tell you so?" Delia resumed, then to butter me up, "Jake's done a great job." She moved a hand toward the shoes, but Bill Trufield swatted her away.

"Don't touch them directly," he cautioned. "We don't want to rub any oils off our fingers." Delia was a bit put out, but she nodded in agreement. "Oils and other contaminants," Bill said. "Contaminants may be our biggest nemesis."

He didn't seem to care that Clue and I had been putting our hands all over those shoes for years. It was always with respect, of course, but those shoes had been touched more than a new baby in a house full of spinster aunts. Despite concerns, I sat there quietly. I guess part of me hoped that Bill would tell Delia the shoes weren't worth so much, after all. Life would have been hard for a few days, but she'd have been fine in the end.

I should have known better. "I know a guy in Washington," Bill continued, "who can get us a line on potential buyers. He says the market's a little slow on clothes memorabilia right now, but given the special circumstances, these should make a good profit."

"You know a guy?" I said.

"Well, I got a phone number. But the guy who answered sounds on top of things."

"How much profit?" Delia said.

"Thousands. Who knows? Maybe there'll be a bidding war."

"A bidding war," Delia repeated, falling in love with the words. "So should we list them on the internet?"

"The internet? Lord, no. That would bring unwanted attention. We have to be discrete. Indiscretion may be our biggest nemesis."

"Don't forget contaminants," I prompted.

Bill purported to think again then laid a hand on his chest. "The best thing, if you don't mind, might be for me to take them with me. It would be easier to make inquiries that way."

They turned in my direction. I wanted things to stop. But the look on Delia's face said that, by declining, I would betray not only everything that had passed between us in our relationship but also everything that she had ever believed about love generally. I couldn't pull the rug out from under her like that. "You can have one of them," I said.

"Take the left one," Delia said immediately. "It's got the stains. They're more personal."

Bill agreed. He removed a handkerchief from his back pocket and grabbed the shoe at the top of the heel, then slid it into a gallon Ziploc bag that Delia held open, both of them careful not to brush the shoe against any part of their skin. At the door there was talk. I could hear them behind me, all "gold mine" and "it's just a small percentage" and "what would we do without you." Bill promised to have word to us within a week. He said that these things moved fast once the dogs caught the scent, and he and Delia both laughed a little. When she came back, she looked like she'd proven something to me. "Well," she said, then headed into the bedroom, leaving me to consider the lone right shoe as I polished off the rest of the pimento sandwiches.

• • •

When I was nine years old, I started running away from home. At least that's what I called it. Each day after school, I'd pack a knapsack with clothes and some food then pick a direction to start walking.

I'm not sure why I did it or what I was looking for. I never lasted more than an hour before heading back to the house. By the time my father got home from the base, I'd long since stationed myself in the kitchen, pretending to do homework. If he suspected anything, he never said so.

It stopped as quickly as it started. One day I'd followed the train tracks as far as Walthall then turned east toward I-95. There was a gas station just short of the highway, with an RV parked to one side, nuzzled up to the air and water pumps. It was newer than Clue's, and white instead of yellow, and there was no junk inside save for two fishing magazines on the table and three spotted bananas hung with a rubber band from one of the cabinet handles. But I was hopeful when I saw the old man in the driver's seat, his head propped on one hand above a map of Virginia, until the second he stood and turned around. "Well," he said, his voice friendly but expecting an answer, "what do you want?"

I don't remember the order of things said after that, but I know that I told him about my parents and Clue. We split one of the bananas, and he found a couple of Cokes in the fridge, then told me that his name was Dale Sherman and that, after his wife had died, he'd bought the RV so he could drive around to see things and meet people. He said his wife had always wanted to do that, and he figured he owed it to her.

He took me home right after. I didn't know street names and must have signaled a half-dozen wrong turns, but he went on patiently, heaving the RV around cul-de-sacs and back streets until I found a landmark that looked familiar. He shook my hand firmly when he put me out at home, like he meant it. "I suppose you'll tell my father," I said.

"I suppose I don't have to," he replied. We looked at my front door, an unexpected silence, then he put a hand on my shoulder and said, "Sometimes you just have to bear up, you know?"

I hadn't understood what he meant at the time, but considering the lone shoe left on the card table in my living room, the idea was starting to make sense. Truth to tell, I could have used Mr. Sherman right then. What I needed was someone to look at my situation from all sides and tell me that I was right to feel a little wrong about where I was headed. Things had seemed okay when they were just me and Clue, the shoes a sort of novelty, and nobody getting hurt. But I feared Delia had set a big rock in motion, the only question being how much damage it would do before finding the bottom of the hill.

I tried to tell her as much on a Tuesday. We were eating Arby's sandwiches off of TV trays, the shoe between us like a houseguest refusing to make conversation. After Bill Trufield's visit, Delia had stopped cooking, saying that she had to prepare herself for "better things." I was halfway through my Big Montana, and there were a couple of personal apple pies waiting for us, with scoops of frozen custard melting over the tops in neat white pools. "Deel," I said, "about the shoes."

"Bill said it won't be long. He's got some nibbles."

"Yeah, well . . . I guess I'm thinking more down the road."

Long term conversation always caught Delia's interest. She pushed her curly fries to one side and leaned forward. "How so?"

Suddenly I wished I'd planned a speech rather than jumping right in. "It's just the whole idea. I mean, maybe the shoes *should* be somewhere other than my closet. But I was thinking more like a museum. Or maybe we should give them back to the family. It seems right."

She tucked her tongue beneath her upper lip for a second, then said, "Do you really think those people give a damn about you? I mean, do you think if they had to choose between saving your life and picking up a nickel they wouldn't go home five cents richer? That's just how wealthy people are."

"I guess. But it's more about us, isn't it?"

"Damn right it's about us. That's what I've been saying all along." She slid out of her chair, came over, and got on her knees in front of me. "What good would it do to put those shoes in a museum where people will gawk at them, taking pleasure in somebody else's pain? It's like those folks who stare at car accidents." She took my hand. "Better that they go to somebody who really appreciates them—who's willing to show that appreciation with some cash up front. And better for us, too. Those shoes can help. You see that, right?"

"I see things have changed."

"Things have changed?" She stared at me like I'd landed a lawn-dart between her eyes. "Of course they've changed. I want to marry you, Jake. I want kids. Life ain't nothing but change, and it's high time you admit it." I looked away from her, but she held my hand even tighter. "Some nights," she continued, "I wake up thinking about that religion where you're headed to heaven or hell from the day you're born. There's nothing you can do about it either way. God loves you, or He doesn't. You know the one I mean?"

I shook my head.

"Well, it's an old one. Anyway, I never could get that idea out of my head, where we're all stuck on our paths. And it's a sad thing, Jake. It's a terrible, sad thing." She reached up one hand and turned my chin so that I was looking right into her wet, brown eyes. "Those shoes made me see different. That's all."

There's a line between hope and foolishness, I guess, and honestly I had no idea where Delia stood relative to it. It was funny how she brought up religion, because in the end it was a question of belief, and maybe she was crazy to put stock in ideas that she'd never gotten proof of, but on the other side, all I had was a pair of shoes and an old man who'd been in my life for a couple of months total—and that was a generous count. Right then, I felt like I knew my father a little better. I'd always thought he hated Clue because Clue had never been a real Daddy to him, never played ball or taught him to fish or showed him what good things in life there might be. But maybe it was the opposite. Maybe Clue was nothing *but* hope and promise and potential, just enough to make Dad want to believe, and then he was gone again, leaving a big hole behind him. Maybe Clue was Dad's only evidence of a better, impossible world. And what a son-of-a-bitch he was to make people want things that way. Either he stood for God's honest truth, or he was the biggest liar that ever existed, and there was no way to tell which. That was a religion of sorts, though I doubted Delia would see it. So we stayed there a long time, her head in my lap and my hand through her hair, the pools of frozen custard melting into lakes that overflowed their containers onto the TV trays. And I decided it was sad how most relationships die, not for lack of understanding, but for the words to express it.

• • •

It turned out that Bill Trufield's Washington contact wanted a better look at the shoe, so the next Thursday Bill and Delia shipped it from the law office to a Silver Hill address. Bill's plan was to have it back by Monday, along with a statement of how much money we could expect to make. All weekend, he and Delia debated by e-mail the merits of selling the shoes individually or as a set.

I'd been warned that Bill would stop by the house after work on Monday. Through the front window I could see him coming up the walk with Delia, who was smiling but looked a little wrung out. She motioned to the FedEx box tucked under Bill's left arm. In response, he flapped his right arm up and down a little, like a big flightless bird with ambition.

"What's the good word?" I asked as they came in.

"Don't know," Bill said. He put the FedEx box on the card table and pulled off the tape, then sent a few packing peanuts swaying to the floor as he pulled out the shoe. It was still wrapped in a plastic bag, and Bill was again careful to use a handkerchief when he removed it and set it next to its mate. He pulled an envelope out of the box, then dropped the box beneath the table. "We thought everybody should hear the verdict at the same time."

"We owed it to you," Delia added, which made me feel kind of good.

Bill gouged one finger beneath the seal of the envelope and started to tear, then thought better of it and passed it to Delia. She held it in both hands, shaking a little, until Bill cleared his throat louder than phlegm should have required.

"Right," Delia said. She unfolded the letter and started reading to herself.

"Out loud," Bill prompted.

"I'm getting there." She scanned the paper a little faster. "It says the shoes would have been the right style for Kennedy. And size 10C, that's right too." She looked up at us and smiled a little, and Bill made a twirling motion with his hand that told her to hurry to the good part. There was a moment while she was staring at the letter when I still thought everything might be okay, but then she turned to the second page, then back to the first, then held them side by side, not saying anything.

"Well?" Bill said.

"They say the *style* is right." She folded the letter and handed it to Bill. "But the brand we have wasn't made until 1965. That's two years too late."

"Well, he was the *President*," Bill said. "Maybe he had shoes made special. Or maybe he got the new brands ahead of time."

Delia walked over to one of the armchairs and bent her knees until she was sitting. She wrapped both arms around her middle and stared at the shoes, like they were an idea she couldn't quite get her brain around. "They're worthless," she said.

"Worthless?" Bill Trufield echoed. He snatched the letter open but did not look at it long enough to actually read it. Instead, he folded it and tossed it to one side, then shoved his hand into the left shoe, no longer worried about contaminants, and lifted it from the table. "What about the blood?" he said. He pointed the toe at my nose. "What about the *blood?*"

"Bill," I said, "maybe now's not the right time for this."

For a second, he seemed unsure of where he was, his eyes frogging out of his already puffy face. But just as quickly, the crimson drained back into his body. He wagged the shoe a little, then smiled as he let it fall. "I know what this is," he said. "They're trying to lower the price on us. We have to play it cool." He nodded repeatedly. "They'll come around when they see we mean business. I know a fish when I smell one, Jake, and the fleet is in."

I guess at some level I'd been prepared for the news, and as much as I wanted to believe that in his moment of greatest sincerity Clue would never have lied to me, I also knew that truth and sincerity were separate matters to him. I picked up the letter and took my time reading it. "I don't think they're interested," I said when I had finished.

"Well, that doesn't mean anything," Bill insisted. "There are other buyers. Shoot, I'll march back to your computer right now and sell them on the internet, if that's what you want."

I creased the letter tight and handed it to him. "Good night, Bill." I could tell he wanted to say something else, but he took stock of me and Delia and put a clamp on it. As he started toward the door, I felt sound escaping my mouth. "Bill."

"Yeah?" He whipped around, his face hopeful.

"Leave the shoe."

"Oh." He pulled it gently off his hand and set it on the table. "Right."

When the door had clicked shut, I went over to Delia and sat down on the floor in front of her. She was still looking at the shoes, so I did too. We sat that way for a good while, neither of us saying a word, the world outside drifting from dim to full dark. Finally I felt her move a little. "We can't go on like this," she said. "We're not what I once thought."

The two small lamps in the room were trying to fight off the night. I noticed things that I usually wouldn't, a string of spider web floating away from a lampshade, whorls of dust that spun through the light even though the air didn't seem to be moving. "They're still JFK's shoes," I said.

"No, they're not. You read the note."

I took a deep breath. "I mean that they've always been JFK's shoes to me. Other people don't matter. They can still be JFK's shoes if we want."

I turned around to catch her almost smiling, but it wasn't necessarily a happy smile. "That," she whispered, "is the dumbest thing you've ever said." She slipped her legs past my shoulder and pushed on the armchair to get herself moving.

I didn't speak until she was fully across the room. "Give it tonight at least." She swiveled her head so that we could hold each other's eyes for a second then passed into the bedroom and closed the door behind her.

I waited until it was quiet, then another half-hour to make sure she was sleeping. Outside, the night sky was so black it seemed purple. There were stars. Car sounds from the highway slapped through the trees, but it was a work night, so folks had mostly turned in. I was almost surprised by the sound of the truck engine, and I waited to make sure no lights came on in the house before backing away.

I put on JFK's shoes sitting in the bleachers of the high school stadium, having squeezed through a gap in the fence that had been there since before I was a freshman. It was chilly out, sweatshirt weather, but the air coming off the football field smelled like spring already, damp and full. I let my body bounce a little on the track, warming up before starting. The shoes were a size small for me, but with the laces loosened, they felt all right.

I thought about some things as I walked, like how it was odd that Clue had gone through an entire war—the biggest war—without a scratch. And even Kennedy, how he was saved by a coconut, and came home to a life that had been meant for his brother. Then Dallas.

But mostly I just walked, letting my feet feel the shoes around them, the track beneath. I tried to be unhappy, figuring I had a right, but somehow I couldn't bring myself to it. In the moonlight, my shadow seemed to pack itself into each shoe as my feet swung one past the other. I crossed the finish line once, then crossed it again, then stopped counting the laps. I knew that my legs would give out eventually, or my body would start to feel hollow, like something had left me without my brain sounding the alert. But that time was a ways off. Now and then, the shoes made a sound like breathing, the only sound I heard, and I was moving, and for the moment that was enough.

Burn

We caught a witch on 67th Street by the Park and took her downtown for the burning. At first, she claimed we were mistaken. She yelled to the crowd that she was a public school teacher from Brooklyn, then pretended to list her students—Stan, Phil, Bobby, Wilhemena. Well-versed in witch chicanery, we ignored her completely.

The Mayor was one of our boys. Though stingy with parade permits, he was always looking for a winning sports team or good public burning. He sent the police to protect us from the paparazzi and German tourists. Watching the policemen link arms, the witch noted cryptically how they resembled an ink-blue wave on which one might ride until one ultimately sank.

We passed the shops on Fifth Avenue. We passed St. Patrick's Cathedral. At Rockefeller Center, someone had the great idea to put the witch on skates, so we did. We expected the fires of Hell to melt through the ice and leave the witch humiliated in a puddle. Instead the witch did a few laps around the rink, gaining speed. She performed a toe-loop and a single-axel. When we lifted her up to resume our march, our accountant, Bernie, pointed out that next time we should devise a test with a smaller margin of error.

Of course there were problems. From windows along our route, protestors threw drywall, glass bottles, and ACLU cards. The cards were most dangerous, since the protestors had watched several Ninja movies and learned how to flick their wrists powerfully. It was rumored that a well-thrown card could split an oak door in half. Still, we were the majority and would do what we liked until we became the minority. Larry, our chiropractor, took down the names of protestors for future expeditions.

We waved to the students in Washington Square then stopped for chow mein in Chinatown. Near Mulberry Street, someone gave the witch a cannoli. By the time we reached City Hall, the pavement was already littered with important documents that had been shredded for confetti. Strapping the witch to the stake, we were lost in a blizzard of lawsuits, quarterly reports, and subpoenas.

The witch did not want to die. She worried about Johnny Tuckwiller, who still had not mastered his multiplication tables. She lamented Cheryl Moretti, whose parents drank and who never had a proper lunch. The Mayor would not listen. He told the crowd that witches were a scourge on the city. He prepared to blow his gold whistle. The men with the lighter fluid backed away. The men with the torches made ready.

But then the whole thing was disrupted by red lights, water, and the clanging of bells. The fire chief declared the street a public hazard. He said the paper would burn like Tokyo, 1945. The Mayor dramatically pretended to strike a match, but he knew the fire chief was right. The chief was concerned for our welfare. "What good does it do to burn witches," he asked reporters frankly, "if you kill yourself in the process?"

What else could we do? We waited until the crowd went home. We considered the witch slumped next to the stake. Oliver, our lawyer, even suggested letting her go. He said there would be other witches and that, truth to tell, sometimes even the most civic-minded people mistook public-school teachers for the Devil's servants.

By now it was toward evening, so I said that Oliver was right. I said that the witch seemed like a nice-enough gal, as witches go, and that maybe we had been too hasty. I said that Ruben and Terry and I would make sure she got home okay.

Not that I meant a word of it. Once a thing has gone so far, it simply must get to its end. After the others left, we three bound the witch with streamers until she looked like a papier-mâché ball. Later, in the darkness, we carried her head-and-foot to the East River. Above us the slivered moon clung to the sky like a discarded toenail in a carpet. The witch groaned as we released her.

Watching her fall, Ruben wondered if she would float, as witches were rumored to do in our histories. Unlike our ancestors, we didn't hang around to find out.

Some Notes on the War

There should have been more to the war. But away from the actual fighting, on the civilian side, the war was only what we had seen in movies, death and shit—perhaps excitement at the fruitful prospect of death and glory, but only for a short time—then more shit. It was malaise, and when it was not malaise, it was combustion, then waiting. Waiting was the only certainty, a feather trapped inside our clothing. It was ennui and anxiety at the same time. Children's voices from the street did not remind us of better days. We knew the war would resume—from the NorthWestEastSouth, from the direction of the people who didn't like us, whose armies were in the same business as ours. And though we often heard that our armies were the better armies and our leaders the better leaders, it was a tricky business. We sometimes thought about the people who did not like us, who by some sleight of ancestry or acumen were not soldiers but mere people like ourselves, waiting somewhere else. We wondered what we were waiting for. We slouched past Olivier the barber, who blasted war news from his shop radio and reminded us that the soldiers' business was our business too. He was not wholly wrong. But perhaps not to be reminded by Olivier, we all wore our hair longer those days, letting it digest our ears. The war was a tiresome business—even when our leaders called it a necessary and sometimes triumphant business. We never conceded their point. We said only that the war was many things, but above all business.

• • •

Lucretia and I were in love during the war, which is not to say we truly loved, only to admit the romance of being in love during a war. It felt natural, inevitable, a commission of self to the most basic impulses. We screwed all over the city: phone booths, public restrooms, the river-bank. When we rolled beneath the rose bushes in the park, we toppled into other screwing couples and bounced back, an echo of flesh. The other couples were in love like us, in war love. We talked about the possibility of our dying, and it made the loving sweeter. Such feelings passed for happiness during the war, and everyone was happy in his or her own way. Even the whores were happy, and the whoremongers, and the whore customers, every whore in the war. And when the rose bushes burned into blossom the next spring, we took it as a sign of our purity of instinct. We were attracted to signs during the war. We were looking for things to believe in.

• • •

Most days the baby would not eat her peas, and because we had to be frustrated by something during the war, Lucretia and I chose the baby. The baby was learning to talk, and each day she added a new word to her vocabulary. *Peas. Horse. Window. Poop. No. Lie.* We told ourselves it was merely a phase and that, when the war ended and fresh vegetables again rolled in from the countryside, the baby would eat. The baby repeated each new word for hours at a time, until the word ceased to be a word and became merely noise—then became something else. *Art. War. Desire. Flesh. Gestalt.* It occurred to us that the baby knew something we did not. But it was an idea we presumed to haunt most new parents, a fear that our children would evolve beyond us. We ate our peas with dramatic spoon flourishes, and rubbed our stomachs contentedly, and hummed our satisfaction like motorboats into the baby's ear. We played "Open up for the choo-choo." Through the night, the baby mumbled like a train. *Complicit complicit complicit complicit complicitcomplicitcom. . . .*

• • •

The bombs dropped by the enemy were not big bombs. Each morning we woke to find things missing—a street lamp, a steeple, a public toilet—as if the enemy were simply reminding us that, as in all experience, there is risk. We assumed there was something beyond the risk as well, something oblique and desirable, but the bombs took our assumptions into account. Sometimes they would not obliterate a house so much as mush it like a potato. Sometimes a bomb could even drop a house in such a way as to leave people trapped inside with the usual amenities—food, water, bed. Such people had books and light, though no one ever claimed to read while waiting for the rescuers to churn through the rubble. Indeed, they claimed, the scariest part of the ordeal was the way that their lives inside the ruined house resembled their lives outside it. When Vasily's house was bombed, it took two days to reach him. We found him on the toilet beside a copy of Fessprod's *De Nugarum Natura* that he'd been threatening to read for a decade. Aside from a bit of constipation, he seemed perfectly normal, unperturbed. He blinked twice in the sunlight and stared around at each of our staring faces. "Right," he concluded, "you've come for dinner, then?"

• • •

It wasn't just the peas, but the peas were the most obvious problem. They were the alpha and omega of the baby's culinary aversions. If we could only get the baby to eat her peas, we reasoned, perhaps only a single pea, then surely the floodgates of her appetite would be loosed, and she would demand fare of all kinds: apples borscht lasagna knitsches poi rhubarb canned ham. Not that we had any of those things, but the baby's desire would have been enough. The baby's desire would have made her part of this world and not part of the uneasy-beyond-the-solitary-womb world in which she seemed to exist. We felt guilty, fearful that we had made her this way, and we tried to make her feel guilty in turn. We told her that the soldiers at the front line, fighting and dying so she might enjoy her peas, would have killed for peas themselves. She echoed us, *Soldiers kill for peas,* though expressed no greater interest in the vegetables before her. Her ribs were showing, and she ran her fingers across them repeatedly, a strum of flesh, an unheard chord.

• • •

To make things seem normal, Lucretia and I took long walks by the river. Not that we remembered long walks before the war. The war had dragged on so long that everything about our lives, even memories, seemed connected to it in some way. Beyond the war there were only the lives we invented. We motioned to the flattened buildings. *Here,* we pretended, *is the theater where we met during a matinee of "First Fox-trot in Brisbane." And here is the cheese shop where we bought our Ruddy Stilton in ten-pound wheels. Here is the dog catcher, and here is the alley where the dogs hid. Here is the post office. Here is the burlesque show. Here is the home of the woman who made tassels for the burlesque show. Here is the yarn shop, then the green grocer. Here is the apothecary who would send a boy around to Ernest Fessprod's house with bicarbonates. Here is the church, and the mortician, and the Ministry of Taxation, and the bricklayer's guild, and the dance club, and the apartment where we lived during our university days. Here is a stone that we once warmed and placed under our bed on a cold winter night. It came from a wall that once held out barbarians. Here is the wall that once held out barbarians. Here are the dirty children who scuttle across it easily.*

• • •

The bombs dropped by the enemy were not fast bombs. They descended on purple satin parachutes, and if we looked up, we would generally have time to race beyond their radius. Still there were people who did not avoid the bombs, perhaps because they were slow people, but just as often because they had succumbed to the doctrine that bombs hitting people were a necessity of war. Regrettably, the bombs did not always detonate. Sometimes they just crushed their victims. Sometimes they opened to disperse leaflets that warned us about our hopeless situation or advertised a 2-for-1 special at a dry cleaner in enemy territory. Sometimes, to prove they were civilized, the enemy would send bombs that, upon impact, would unfold into elaborate tea services with scones and petit fours, piping hot Darjeeling or Earl Grey, and place cards that read *To the infidels, with our compliments.* Our government reminded us of the consequences of forbidden fruit. They retaliated with whatever missiles they could muster: Victrolas of foot-tapping old-timey songs, beef tenderloin with béarnaise, several live poets who rocketed off as ambassadors armed with leather-bound copies of their collected works and little chocolate medallions wrapped in glittering foil.

• • •

We never named the baby. It seemed pointless and too hopeful at the same time, an act of hubris. The baby's self-starvation was not the only thing bothering us. She made coal etchings of Etruscan temples described by a turtle in one of her books. She crafted variations of minor Czech etudes on a toy glockenspiel that lit up and played "You Are the Pot at the End of My Rainbow" when the right button was depressed. Concerned, we took her to Ernest Fessprod, who was rumored to be the most intelligent man in the city because he was old and blind. Ernest filled his house with thousands of clocks and went barefoot day and night. When the wind blew a clock from its shelf, Ernest could tell the exact time at which it had stopped merely by stepping on it. He believed strongly in the dictum that history repeats itself, else why would men craft clocks with only circular faces. When Lucretia broached the subject of digital clocks, he answered with a rambling treatise on plant fertilizer and dramatic unities. He picked up the baby and waited until she retched on his double-vested seersucker jacket. *There is always an answer,* he reminded us with self-assurance, *even if we never find it.*

• • •

To be sure, some people supported the war. They traveled the city looking stern and, when needed, found someone not as stern as themselves to rap about the ears in an act of castigation. Such attacks were minor, so those of us in the not-so-stern crowd generally let them pass. We were not without demonstration, however. We carried candles to the medieval keep where our leaders had lodged themselves and walked around the moat, singing songs about peace and self-expression and slow-burning candles. Several times, our leaders posted a representative atop the walls to remind us that only the war could bring a permanent peace. In response, Manuel started a rumor that the government was run by wrestlers and men who had failed the auto mechanic's exam, but it was soon overtaken by Enrico's sentiment that the government was run by personal injury lawyers and angry hamsters. When we threw our candles into the moat, our leaders moved cannons to the wall as a preventative measure. From inside came the sound of moiling dogs, and the representative backed away, hands outstretched as if to push something down, saying *Thanks again for coming glad we're on the same page.*

• • •

And because we were desperate, we feared that we could never, after the war, create lives for ourselves that felt so essential. More than once Lucretia turned to me in bed to suggest that the war, in its opaque way, had done us a favor by revealing us to ourselves. And I have to say that a sense of urgency, though not excitement, hung so palpably on the air that I could bring myself to orgasm simply by touching the naked backside of Lucretia's left thigh while she slept. And I remember thinking each time that I had never felt so aroused, that I had never seen this woman in this precise way. And because I always wanted to see her this way, I would take a notebook and pencil from the desk and, holding a candle over her thigh, attempt to transcribe what I had witnessed that made me feel so inspired. And it was a great disappointment to me when all I could manage to write was *Lucretia's leg, pale, with lines* and to know that on every other page were the words *Lucretia's leg, pale, with lines.* And that when I stepped outside, the stirred emotions would dissipate back into the tedium of the war, as if the war were teasing me with pleasures that it would always take away. As if the war knew that I would drift back inside to fall into bed next to Lucretia who, stirred from sleep though never quite awake, would turn my direction and murmur *Who are you?* And I would not respond for fear of waking her fully and having her realize—in that first shock of waking recognition—that she could not answer her own question, and neither could I.

• • •

To make things seem normal, Ernest recounted our most ancient stories. *Remember the Achons,* he said, *and their siege of the city of Tryst—how the Trystites had stolen the sacred jam of the Achons and for ten years eaten it mockingly atop the walls of their city. Only then did the wise Achon general Odius place several bags of fancy bread atop a jackass and send it through the gates of Tryst, where the Trystites ate the bread with their jam, and grew ill, and hurried to the lavatory, and returned only to discover that the jackass was Odius himself, who had not shaved for several days in preparation for the role. And recall how Odius had allowed the other Achons through the Trystite gates, and then there had been much fighting and slaughter and gnashing of teeth and breast-beating and hair-pulling and groin kicks and rabbit punches and atomic knee drops and wailing women and overturned jam jars. And high atop the walls of Tryst the Achon hero Axetogrind had chased the Trystite hero Halliwell, with his long-flowing mane, on unicycles, around and around the walls, until Halliwell caught his hair in the spokes of Axetogrind's wheel, and Axetogrind kept pedaling until the hirsute Halliwell was no more, and thus was the death of Axetogrind's boon companion, Propitious the Understudy, avenged. And Axetogrind cut a small lock of Halliwell's hair for each of the Achon champions, but still there was woe, for never had so much jam been spilt, and now there was no jam for anyone, and the Trystite women were not as attractive as in legend, and it would take another ten years for the Achons to return to Achonius, because no one had brought a map. And thus,* Ernest concluded, as he glanced at the frowning baby, *we see the truth about war, whatever it is.*

• • •

The bombs dropped by the enemy were not smart bombs. By the end of things, we could point in another direction or simply tell them they had gotten the wrong address, and they would go away. Once, a bomb knocked on our door dressed as a salesman of chocolates, but we pretended to be lactose-intolerant, which put him off for a while. Or maybe this was all a dream. I cannot recall exactly. It seems to me now that some bombs did go off, and metal and flames and human limbs were flung in every direction, and once I stepped from my door to find Mrs. Ogobe with a piece of bomb that bore the enemy's insignia, rubbing it in a pile of her husband's remains, saying *Bad bomb, bad bomb!* It was then I walked down to the river, stepped onto the water's surface, and remembered the trick I had known as a boy that kept me from plunging through the surface into the deep. All of my friends had played the trick at one time or another, a trick that the war had made us think impossible. But I remembered it as soon as I saw my feet atop the shimmering carpet, and at the river's end was the sea, and I knew that if I followed the sea as far as it went, I could get to a place without war, which was the one place that the war had made us forget. And many nights thereafter, waking in a sweat, I had to remind myself that it was not just a dream, even though there were Lucretia's pale lined thighs beside me and the baby's lexicon drifting in from the other room. And I would go to the baby and tell her what she needed to know about the river, that I would not blame her, that we could all just walk away. To which she waved her hand before her sleep-draggled face, as if warding off a ghost, or a father who has kissed her one too many times, and murmured *But we don't.*

• • •

In the end, the bombs gave up first. They were tired, I suppose, and had seen so many of their comrades frittered away—so many of their younger, better peers—that they finally gave in to their own inadequacies and ceased to be what our leaders wanted. Lucretia and I would see them when we walked hand in hand by the bomb yard. By then Lucretia had asked that we give ourselves over to a new Platonism and performed mystical ceremonies with willow branches and sage flakes to return her body to a virgin state. I still had urges but considered the way that the first baby had turned out and decided that she was perhaps right. In the bomb yard, the young lieutenants lined the bombs in rows and reviewed their faults for the general. *This one is not big enough,* they said. *And this one is not loud enough. And this one has become a bloody pacifist. This one is pedantic, and this one speaks only Japanese, and this one tells boring stories about a simpler time. This one thinks it is funny but isn't. That one there, as you can see, paints corporate logos over its body, and the one next to it claims to be Hans Dittmeier, a tourist from Dresden. The one to your left waxes philosophic after only one glass of wine, and the one to your right thinks you are a silly, silly man. Most of the others just keep to themselves and play bridge when they have the chance. And the ones you cannot see are the ones that have gone missing. There are more of those each day. We're not sure what to say about them.*

· · ·

We could have kept on, with guns or sticks or fists. But gradually everyone lost interest. Soldiers drifted back from the front, first in pairs or trios, then by the busful. They seeped into the city's arteries, though what they did specifically I cannot say. I never met a person who claimed to have been a soldier, and it might have been tempting, amid the silence of no bombs, to assume that we might return to our normal lives, except I never heard any person speak about a normal life as if no one had contemplated such a thing except for our leaders, who soon took up the issues of genetically enhanced tomatoes and lesbian adoptions. Lucretia and I separated, not slowly but one morning after breakfast, when neither of us could remember why we'd come together in the first place. We sent the baby to a school for the gifted in Devon where her musical talents could be developed fully. She is presently composing a suite of bassoon miniatures devoted to animals she's seen run over by motorcars, but her house-mother claims she is eating well. It is a small victory to keep close to my heart. On other matters, I have heard rumors that the war never really ended. There was no treaty, and there have been no signs of the generals, who are likely in bunkers somewhere, planning the next wave. It doesn't matter. I keep Lucretia's new phone number in my front pocket in case the war fires up again, but were the bombs to resume, I suspect any warm body would do. She now runs a hostel for interpretive dancers. I have taken a job as Ernest Fessprod's personal assistant, where I follow him with a small legal pad, noting everything that he says. Our lives are methodical and empty, but I devote several leisure hours each week to a newly formed debating society whose sole object is to determine whether or not things were better during the war. Like many peers, I am in the undecided camp. During our afternoon sessions, when the sunlight awls through the windows, and the small table fans are not enough to keep us cool, I imagine myself striking out for enemy territory and telling the first person I find what a great ninny he was for pitching us into this state of affairs. But then I wonder if ninny-baiting weren't what started the war to begin with. I don't ever mention the other thing, the part about the river and walking away, even though some of my erstwhile colleagues were themselves once children and might remember. I do not know why walking on water is a trick only children can perform and not just children but only the very young, just removed from infancy into the great swales of language that make all things possible, who know the words but not yet exactly what to do with them. I suspect it is less a matter of belief than balance, the right amount of fluid in the inner ear, though here too I may be wrong. I can only confirm that when I pass mirrors today I am surprised to see the veins of white that marble my beard, and I can say from experience that no one listens to old men. And I do not know whether to be happy or sad at this fact, to scream at young people that even an unfulfilled life can be its own genius. Or else to tell them just go, go, take the keys and drive—and don't worry about curfews or ontology or road signs warning of badgers: these have mucked things up enough already.

The President's Penis

O f course you didn't want to look, but how could you help looking when it was plastered across every TV in the Western world and even the Christian groups and right-wing PACs were saying that it was needed for an impartial verdict? Face it, you'd been a little curious since the first sketches began to appear in the tabloids and witness-victims started recounting its distinguishing features: a clover-shaped mole near its circumcised tip, a slightly deformed testicle that resembled a human face when viewed from the proper angle. The face was what the prosecutors highlighted after the photos had been taken, tracing its outline with laser-pointers on the House floor and noting how it fit the description given by both the Midwestern secretary and the fast-food clerk: firm-jawed and even angry, like James Cagney in *The Public Enemy*. And despite your conviction that the whole thing was detestable, you entered the debates around the water cooler, saying that it looked nothing like Cagney but more like a tormented Jimmy Stewart in *Mr. Smith Goes to Washington* or in that part of *It's a Wonderful Life* where George Bailey's thinking about jumping off the bridge before the angel shows up. You even dreamed about it: a police line-up in which you were asked to identify the offending member from a group of five, peering through the one-way glass while a fat sergeant who looked like your ninth-grade government teacher,

Mr. Delinsky, ate brie on Saltines and said, "Tell us what we want to know." And finally you thought how all this began not yesterday, not even last year, but a long time ago—like the liberals said, sex and power—and that probably no individual could hope to stop it. Especially with the pictures enlarged as if they were Russian missile sites on your screen, and the defense attorneys saying that the mole obviously looked more like a crucifix than a clover, and the outline of that face beneath a thin layer of skin as if drowning, a face that could have been yours had it not finally seemed so sad to you, sadder than you knew you had ever been.

When the President Prays

1. When the President prays, he tilts his neck slightly to the right so that his head can never be fully bowed. Sometimes he even keeps his eyes open. On TV the President's lips are moving, but because of the discreet placement of the microphones, it is impossible to tell whether or not he is speaking the words of the prayer.

The leader of the opposition considers this a grave issue. Observing the video closely, he says, you can tell that the President's mind is not on salvation, as it should be, but on new plots to bilk the taxpayers out of their hard-earned incomes. Weekly, the opposition leader puts a white envelope in the collection plate where he worships. The envelope has a message printed on it so that other parishioners will never forget what to think about. The wages of sin are death, it says. Honor thy father and thy mother. Vote for B_____. The opposition leader claims that the President listens to music referring to God as a construct and that he eats at restaurants with sacrilegious names.

At his customary seat in the local *Burger Heaven*, the President considers what the opposition leader has said. He remembers reading somewhere how a Poughkeepsie woman found a rusted fish hook in her *Burger Heaven* Patty o' Flounder—this only months after the human finger in the double Bun o' Beef. The finger was made of rubber and probably some kid's idea of a joke. Nonetheless the President urges caution. He places a call to the FDA and thinks about creating a new cabinet post. In his bedroom before sleep, the President prays that he will find neither rusty hooks nor body parts in the Extra Economy Dinners that he orders.

· · ·

2. To keep in shape, the President jogs ten miles in the morning and in the afternoon. On the weekends he plays golf. The President belongs to the same country club as many Congressmen and Supreme Court Justices, as well as Q_____ T_____, the film actor once the nation's "Fitness Czar." Naturally there is some bad blood. The manager of the country club tries to keep the foursomes as spread out as possible, but General H_____ has twice accused the President of hitting into his group, and Rep. G_____ was firmly cudgeled by Secret Service agents, who mistook his habitual slice for an assassination attempt.

The President has yet to break 100, though in media releases he lists his handicap at 13. A true fan of the game, he has visited local high schools to give talks on the character building aspects of golf. He has introduced a bill in Congress that would increase the number of public courses in the inner cities. When local merchants and students come to thank him for his efforts, he offers them each a sleeve of his monogrammed balls.

The President wants to give the impression that all is well. He never mentions the CIA operatives who lurk in tunnels below the fairways and use cameras in the sprinklers to keep track of his ball when it goes out of bounds. There are radar installations behind the ball washers and anti-tank missiles in every tree. For a price, the CIA might be willing to tell what it knows about the President, who tees up his ball in the rough when he thinks no one is watching. Sometimes in a bunker, the President utters a word which might be construed as prayer—though even prayer, he concedes, has its limits. There are things about which even God cannot be convinced to care.

· · ·

3. The President and Mrs. President are joining the Japanese Prime Minister, who is in town on a trade mission, for dinner at a local sushi bar. The President has been studying his intelligence manual diligently and knows how to say "Hello," "Good-bye," and "This is the commode" in Japanese. The last three presidents were notorious for their intolerance of sushi, and this president is no exception. He would rather be at *Burger Heaven,* hooks and all. Yet for the good of the nation he has steeled himself to the dinner's inevitability. Don't blow the blowfish, his staff has advised. He has spent weeks preparing: halibut, tuna, eel, squid, even fugu livers. Lest the Japanese think him weak, the President swears to keep his intestines under control.

At the sushi bar Mrs. President makes conversation with the Prime Minister. She speaks eleven different languages—Urdu and Magyar among them—and holds degrees in sociology and international finance. How to describe Mrs. President? She is 6'3," platinum blond with legs that seem to run the length of her body and a girlish giggle which she dispenses freely while making idle chitchat. Or, she is 5'2" in heels, pale-skinned with flowing dark hair and a drawl that reminds one of a country singer. Or, she is 4'6" seated, her auburn hair pulled tightly into a bun, with glasses as thick as Coke bottles and an IQ of well over 180. She is all things to all men. She is, as the President has long known, exactly what is needed in a president's wife.

Later, while the First Lady sleeps, the President watches the national flag waving on his TV—a Zenith—and listens to the national anthem. He presses one hand to where the raw fish is passing slowly through him and feels unfulfilled. Earlier the Japanese Prime Minster taught him how to shave several strokes off his putting game and heal any pain with a single touch to the middle of the palm. The President takes a Maalox. He prays that the trade talks will go well.

• • •

4. Just beyond the White House lawn, Paolo de Medici owns a stand at which tourists can have their pictures taken with cardboard cutouts of the first couple. The President has spent hours watching Paolo through the chinks in his Venetian blinds. He has sent White House

staff members to have their pictures taken with the cardboard and to listen attentively to the bits of free advice which Paolo dispenses with the photos. "Carpe diem," says Paolo. "Tempus fugit. Nolo contendere." Paolo wears a Reebok on one foot and a Nike on the other, claiming that shoes without a match can be had for next to nothing in the great shoe outlets of America. He says his grandfather reached Ellis Island as a young boy with the idea that shoes in America grew on trees. Paolo prays out loud that the spirit of his grandfather will do something about the Mexican on the next block, who has cardboard cutouts of the city football team's quarterback and the Speaker of the House. Paolo is concerned about the increased influx of foreign nationals to the city as well as what he views as big businesses' conspiracy to circumvent anti-trust law by relocating to foreign countries. He has a certain sympathy for protectionist measures presently on the floor of the Senate though at heart he believes trickle-down economics to be a lie of misers and Austrians. He says that he is a moderate.

The President is writing a song in which Paolo has a number of magical adventures. In the song, Paolo slays dragons and contributes generously to local charities. The President wonders if he should sketch in a harmony line for the Vice President, who keeps a worn copper harmonica in the elastic of his sock. The President is a washtub-bass man himself. Before entering politics, he and the Vice President won numerous Bluegrass contests, though creative differences are now driving them apart. Washtub planted firmly against the Great Seal of the nation, the President strums a few bass notes and sings his refrain:

Paol-o, Paol-o Crockett
King of the Wild Frontier.

The President prays for the day when he will be able to move beyond the walls of his castle so that Paolo may take his picture with one of the cardboard cutouts. The President will show the picture to his friends and relatives, challenging them to say which image is real.

• • •

5. Meanwhile in Kablikistan, the Kablikistani Parliament is trying to prevent the breakdown of its nation into ethnic chaos. Kablikistan was among the republics that broke away from the breakaway Republic of Pozhidikstan—formerly of the Soviet Union. Now circumstances have deteriorated into turmoil. Kablikistan measures just under sixty square miles, land which the native Kablikistanis say was promised them by their grandfather's grandfathers as well as Holy Writ. The Kablikistanis form a 73 percent majority in the Republic and have been incited to riot by Boris Medelyev, the former Olympic power-lifter.

The Kablikistani Party Secretary, a Harvard grad, sympathizes with his countrymen. Yet he cannot simply abandon the rest of the citizenry—the Orthodox Pozhidikstanis, the Amerbanis, the Benzir goatmen in the hills just beyond the capital of Tupu. And what of the missiles? They have been cross-laid in the courtyard according to size, the largest as tall as a farm house, the smallest no longer than a thumb, yet each capable of destroying a city several times the size of Kablikistan. What if they should fall into the hands of the egomaniacal Boris Medelyev? (Medelyev, it should be mentioned, is only three feet tall and missing the limbs of his left side.) Would he be content to clean-and-jerk the missiles in the courtyard, to the awed whispers of his supporters? Or are his plans more diabolical than even the Secretary knows? The Secretary has called for international action. Ten million kronats and a case of vodka to the nation that brings him the remaining limbs of Medelyev.

The President likes vodka, though not as much as bourbon or schnapps. Also, he suspects the First Lady of having an affair with the Vice President. His troops will roll through Kablikistan, disarming the missiles, and he will drink vodka with the Party Secretary while singing Harvard's fight song. The First Lady cannot ignore him then. He will shower her with kronats and take her to the finest restaurant in all of Kablikistan, where they will hang his picture above the door in homage. He will wear his uniform—blue, gold, green—and be just one more man among the troops in their blues and golds and greens. The President prays for a swift victory on all fronts. No fight, he trusts, can go on forever.

• • •

6. For public relations purposes, the members of both parties agree to worship at the same Church. The lines, however, are firmly drawn: the President's party to the left, the opposition to the right (or vice versa, depending on your perspective). The opposition leader is wearing a blue blazer, dress khakis, and a red power tie. The other opposition members dress largely the same. The President's side is a veritable fashion menagerie, bow ties and bobby socks, seersucker vests, cardigans, platform shoes. The President himself wears a pair of Italian loafers which the First Lady recently purchased at a nearby shoe outlet.

As the minister completes his *Pater Noster,* the choir launches into "The Ballad of Paolo." The First Lady and Vice President toast each other with the promised vodka while the opposition leader flings his white envelopes into the air, watches them descend like doves in search of olive branches. The Eucharist is served piping hot with sides of spinach dip and paté. Everyone agrees the bread is the best they've ever tasted.

All except for the President, who is praying—neck tilted, head bowed, eyes wide. The television cameras are humming. The minister thinks how there is something familiar to the President's pose. A slant of morning light stabs the altar, illuminates the holiest of holies lying there. The crowd is awash in the dust of its own benedictions. A woman screams. Somewhere a stone rolls back into place.

My Mother's Lover

My mother took a lover named Richard two years before she died. At the memorial service, he was nothing like I expected: a short pudgy man with bifocals and a receding hairline, early sixties, my mother's age. His houndstooth blazer had faded spots on the elbow patches from where he habitually crossed his arms, as if trying to shield himself from a recurring thought he could not quite escape.

"I teach Western Culture at City College," he told me at the door. We shook hands. He smelled faintly of smoke.

What could I say? I showed him the body. Together we stood above the casket like two children having discovered a secret in the woods. "She was a clean woman," he managed.

"Immaculate," I agreed.

"I could never keep things tidy enough for her."

"She used to make the beds in hotel rooms," I told him, "because sometimes the maids didn't do it right."

He nodded slowly, as if unsure whether or not to agree. In a corner of the room, my father hunched forward in his wheelchair, coughing softly, my two sisters fluttering around him. I tried to think of something to say to Richard, something that could encapsulate how I felt when my mother told me she was moving into the guest room for good—something that sounded like my father's dialysis machine, a song of betrayal and unmet expectations but tinged with gratitude all the same. "We always thought Dad would die first," I finally said.

Richard pursed his lips, arms pulling his jacket tighter around his torso. "I don't understand love or death," he replied, "though I've written books on both."

Around us, flower arrangements lined the mahogany walls of the funeral home, their petals casting bright but distorted reflections. When Richard asked for a few moments alone with my mother, I promised to speak with him at the cemetery, but he never came. The last time I saw him he was standing above her, arms folded, leather patches straining at the elbows. Just then he looked like he belonged there, not a part of the scene but a lone witness to the world beyond us, love killing without discretion even as it remained our only comfort.

Great Myths of Our Time

For R.O., 1996

I n his notebook he wrote:

>   *Mikey, the Life Cereal Boy, drank a Pepsi and ate Pop Rocks at the*
> *same time, and his stomach exploded.*

Of course his friends tried to talk him out of it. "Take a look around you, Jack," Rico began, "the doctors gave Laurence a new prescription just last week, state of the art stuff." "And AZT," Howard pointed out, "we know some people in Atlanta pushing it cheap." "Nevirapine, too," Rico agreed, "next to nothing."

But he had decided. Even though mural painting was great work, the benefits sucked. And maybe he'd been crazy to let his insurance slide, but it wasn't like he'd been on some kind of power trip, thought himself invincible. He'd known the risks well enough and if not HIV, maybe leukemia or emphysema or something. Did the name really matter? (Which of course it did, but he wasn't going to admit that.) Because in the end it was simply a choice he'd made, for better or worse, like the one he was making now. He'd live with it. At least for a while.

"Insurance, shminsurance," Rico continued, "Jack, you *got* to fight." But Howard, a red-haired Irish Catholic who understood all about inevitability, saw how things stood, took his hand, hugged him. And Rico cried a little (and maybe he did too, he couldn't remember later) and they each carried a bag down the stairs and loaded them into his yellow VW bug and Howard said, "Where'll you go?" So he smacked the car and joked, "As far as she'll take me." And Rico said, "Call if you need anything, Triple-A, cash." Though they all knew he'd pulled seven thousand dollars, his life savings, out of the bank just an hour earlier, and Rico ran one hand over his stubbly black hair, his dark eyes hazing over as if seeing all those black-market drugs they would never buy. Pulling away from the curb, he waved and even blew them a kiss, but decided not to call out something glib because he knew he might never see them again.

He stopped only at his sister's Soho apartment to tell her what he was doing. "You're a crazy fucker, Jack," she said at one point, her blond-dyed eyebrows lifting, creasing her forehead. "Just like you to go looking for trouble. Remember when you took that header off the carport? I thought that was the end." She frowned. "You should have died before now." Which was a crazy thing to say, they both knew, but it was Joanne and was in its own way an expression of love. Late for an audition, she kissed him good-bye, told him to write, then on her way out handed him the cordless phone. "Call Mom," she said.

So he did. And he told his mother many things of which all he could later remember was the phrase "to die with dignity," as if that were possible. And he thought what a great line that was, "Die with dignity," a great myth of our time, and how much better it might be to mix up a glass of Pop Rocks and Pepsi and listen to his stomach explode like a geyser, flash of glory death, people telling stories about him for decades. But then he remembered how he'd seen Mikey on a talk show just last month and that whole scam dying thing. "What a riot," Mikey had said, "just another show biz myth." So maybe he couldn't die with dignity, but he'd damn well try. And when his mother made him promise to fly back when the real pain started, he didn't have the heart to tell her that pain came in various forms—that it had already "started"—but instead made her another empty promise which in his love probably meant something after all. Then from his bag he withdrew the living will form that he'd bought at the bookstore and left a signed copy on Joanne's table to match the one he'd given Howard earlier, shoving several blank copies back into his bag. And his mother said, "Let me know if you find your father out there." And he thought again how people say the craziest things at a time like this.

But then again, maybe death gave everyone the right.

• • •

In Cleveland he wrote:

Ozzy Osbourne bit the head off a live bat during a concert then hung a midget on stage.

And him with nothing but show tunes. Jesus H. Christ, how cliché. Plus the saddest part: they weren't even his. Ever since Joanne had landed that bit part in *Show Boat*, she'd trashed his car with Broadway tapes *du jour*, driving from audition to audition. Looking around the interior, he felt a strange satisfaction that she would get the car when he was gone. She almost had squatter's rights to it now.

He dumped the tapes into a trash can outside an Ohio Denny's: *Annie Get Your Gun, Forum, Cats, Grease, Chicago, The Fantastiks, Sunset Boulevard.* He kept *Aspects of Love*, though for what reason he couldn't say, then stockpiled on anthologies from the fifties and sixties at the Rock 'N' Roll Hall of Fame. He was humming "Tutti Frutti" when he dropped an armload of cassettes onto the counter, laughed at himself, then made the clerk's eyes bug out when he paid from a wad of hundred-dollar bills. Two full shopping bags later, he finally took the tour and got a British woman to snap a picture of him in a pelvis-thrust before the Elvis exhibit, then took one of her in front of The Shirelles. He convinced her to do a duet of "Momma Said" and even got her to dance for several Chinese spectators with camcorders. Someone in back asked when they were going on tour, and he yelled that he already was.

Driving through the Midwest, he watched family farms and strip malls run together in a blur of pavement. He grew tired easily— fatigue had been his first clear symptom—so he sang along with Ritchie Valens and Buddy Holly to stay alert, and thought how dying wasn't much of a way to live. Okay, maybe refusing treatment wasn't the best idea, but he would die fast, wouldn't he? Fast . . . Fast . . .

Faster, maybe that was the word he was looking for, all things being relative. AIDS, he said to himself, said it again, an innocuous little word, almost made him laugh the pain away. He had gone to the rallies with Rico, the parades, and felt the same stir of righteous anger as everyone else when Howard reported how A.G. Shapiro, VP of Operations at the bank, had asked him to remove the red ribbon from his lapel because it wasn't in keeping with their corporate image. Still, he wondered, was AIDS so much worse? His grandfather, his mother's father, had lingered for months with throat cancer, lost his voice, gone on oxygen, fallen into bed one day never to get back up. In the end they fed him with a needle through a tube, and his mother learned how to tap his arms for unspent veins to put in the IV, and he watched his grandfather become more machine than man, bag of tubes, liquid food that trickled straight into his throat, a larger tube running into the colostomy bag at the other end. He imagined one big tube running right through the old man that connected the tubes between.

It couldn't be that bad. Right? Not if you didn't fight it, if you let nature take its course. Not if you died with dignity.

• • •

Near Fort Wayne he scribbled:

Baseball, hot dogs, apple pie, and Chevrolet.

The living will weighed down his portfolio. He took it out and read it from time to time while driving faster than he had ever driven, surprised at his audacity, at the car's urgency. "Damned if I knew she had it in her," he told the Indiana cop, who pulled him over just before the Illinois border. He took the citation with a polite nod, then withdrew one of the copies of the will that he had not yet signed, signed it, then asked the officer to sign in the space marked Witness. "You need two people to sign this, son," the officer told him, as if even diseases should be made official. "God's watching," he replied, "that's enough." To which the cop, scribbling his name, said, "I suppose, but I'm still not taking back that ticket."

In Chicago, he sat through a daytime double-header at Wrigley

Field and remembered how Rico had mourned the day they installed lights in the park. Rico was from Chicago and said that Wrigley was the only place where he had felt welcome when young, not because he liked baseball so much, but just because the Cubs were so damn bad and it felt so damn good sometimes to be in a place where lost causes were so freely embraced. Sitting in the stands just behind left field, he thought he knew how Rico felt. He waved at the camera when it swung in his direction and imagined Rico and Howard spotting him in the stands (they had paid extra to get WGN in New York). When a fly ball curved in his direction, he leaped up with the rest of the crowd but was brought back to his seat by a clenching pain in his ribs and could only nod when the guy in the Harley T-shirt next to him asked if he was okay. He looked up to see the ball stay fair for a home run and heard the crowd roar when another fan tossed it back onto the field, since it had come off a Pittsburgh bat. Death with dignity, he couldn't help thinking.

The Cubs split the two-fer, 3–10, 2–1. As the fans cleared out, he opened his notebook and wrote "Tinkers to Evers to Chance," lingering over the last word. The guy in the Harley shirt, who'd been playing beer-an-inning through the second game, leaned over and asked, "What's that?" "Great myths of my time," he said, "something to let me know what I'm about." The man's eyes scrunched tight, "You aren't a Pittsburgh fan?" To which he smiled and replied, "I'll get back to you."

Later that night he called his mother and told her he was feeling better. She said, "You'd remember your father, Jack, wouldn't you, if you saw him?"

• • •

In St. Louis he decided on:

Trickle-down economics.

And what was this business with his father? He hadn't seen the man since he was three, couldn't even be sure if the pictures in his head were real memories or fabrications that he'd refined over the years until he believed they were true. Joanne didn't remember squat and liked it that way. "Let the bastard rot, for all I care," she'd say, "walking out on a woman and two kids, what kind of fucker does that?" But Joanne hadn't even been born when their father left. She didn't have memories to contend with, real or imagined.

He convinced a street musician to take several pictures of him with the Gateway Arch in the background, took the film to a one-hour photomat, then drove to just outside the city where he sat on the bank of the Mississippi, eating a cheeseburger and watching small tugboats maneuver barges back and forth between docks. The brown water near his feet made him think of tainted blood, but blood still churning. He threw bits of cheeseburger bun into the air and watched as shrieking seagulls tore the food off the breeze.

His mother had blamed his father for everything, not viciously or even openly, but always. When he was young and did something wrong, she would say, "If only your father had been here." And even though over the years the phrase had fallen away, she kept a look that said more than the words ever could, and he could not bear that look when she turned it upon him, when he declined a graduate art fellowship at NYU to paint murals, when he came home one Thanksgiving with Rodney, his first steady lover. Now AIDS. He couldn't go to see her after that, couldn't stand up to that gray tint which worked its way into her eyes even as she told him how much she loved him, that they would get through this together. The implicit line: "If only your father had been here." But he hadn't been, and who's to say his father's presence would have made a damn bit of difference? Who would have wanted it to?

In Kansas City he ate dinner near the stockyards and, for once, was glad to enjoy a steak in peace. "Red meat kills," Joanne would say, or as Rico mockingly put it, "Carnivore!" Still, eight ounces through the best twenty-ounce T-bone he'd ever tasted, he had to admit to himself that death was liberating in its own way. When he got around to the baked potato, he asked the waitress for extra sour cream.

Back in his hotel room, he flipped through the photos, arranging them in chronological order and writing the date and place on the back of each: the shore of Lake Erie, the golden dome at Notre Dame, the Sears Tower. If he got back to New York, he figured, he would buy a

scrapbook and install the photos along with the pages from the jour-
nal he was keeping. Not that he believed the words and pictures
would automatically come together to tell him something about himself. He had spent hours poring over the scrapbooks at his mother's
house, filled with images of him and Joanne at the beach, letters from
camp, programs from every one of Joanne's plays, certificates of
achievement for each of the County Arts Festivals in which his paintings had appeared during high school. There were locks of hair and
baby footprints and pictures of relatives whom he could not recall. But
none of these ever explained the things he felt like he needed to know.

There was only one picture of his father, and it was not in the
books. His mother kept it on top of her dresser—a scene from his own
front yard—black-and-white image of a sharp-nosed man, thinning
hair slicked down against his scalp, staring at the infant cradled in his
pale bony arms. Holding the baby, the man looks uncomfortable,
pained, as if the small body he supports is in fact some inexplicable
tumor which has bubbled up from his own abdomen. The sun is shin-
ing somewhere to the camera's left. The slant of light gives the illusion
of movement to the several cars parked in the background.

"If only your father had been here." In the hotel room, he could
almost hear the words emanating from the photos that he clutched, tes-
tament to this foolish journey he had undertaken, which could have
only one end. At first, he had seriously considered his mother's suggestion that he find his father. Since he did not know exactly what he
was searching for, one quest seemed as good as another. But in the end
he realized how his mother's idea testified only to her fears come true,
how all the men in her life—father, husband, son—had left her in one
way or another. And he realized how her admonition was not borne
even slightly out of a concern for his welfare, but wholly out of a concern for her own: a last-ditch plea with the universe to return those
things taken from her. To return the two men who never seemed complete when they were with her, but whom she could never stop caring
about.

Bring them home, God. He reflected on the words with contempt
yet understanding. Bring them home: safe, satisfied, whole.

· · ·

Somewhere between Denver and Grand Junction, he scribbled:

Green M&Ms make you horny.

And only God knew how he had tried. At fourteen, there'd been Theresa Mack, who slipped her hand into his pocket at a Connecticut Pitch-and-Putt, supposedly to find his keys. At fifteen, there'd been Sandi Holman, showing him her breasts behind the dumpster at Mike's Bowl America. At sixteen, Angela Stinson, the cheerleader, his chemistry lab partner, blond, leggy—in the bathroom at her birthday party, her parents at some political function, his hand up her skirt, hers down his pants. She went from low moan to high squeal like a Ferrari engine, until he felt ready to die (of fear? of guilt?) about the pain forming in his gut. Not that Angela could tell. He was harder than the steering column on his mother's Buick. But he was sixteen, for Christ's sake—a change in the breeze made him stiff. Was he excited? Sure, but with a feeling that couldn't be described as pain or even nausea. Just absence, a space like bruised fruit carving itself out of his abdomen, his own body betraying him, his own muscles pulling him apart.

(For a fleeting moment he even thought how the disease had brought things full circle—not a disease which attacked his body directly, like cancer, but turned that body on itself—unsexed him, his penis a mere piss spout—his gut turning into a void that would engulf him from the inside out.)

But mostly he just remembered. His mother telling him not to worry, that he just needed to find the right girl. And his trying to fill the emptiness with food: raw oysters, kumquats, green M&Ms—plain and peanut, bags and bags worth. Looking back, he decided that maybe his teenage years hadn't been so bad after all. Not that he ever stopped feeling lonely, but most days his diet kept him too busy puking to worry about it.

He checked into a hotel at Grand Junction, then went on foot with his camera to take pictures of the rivers, the Gunnison and the Colorado. Where the rivers met he made his way to the bank, scooped up a handful of water, sniffed it, splashed his face. There was something meaningful he couldn't quite pin down to the smoothness with which the rivers came together. None of the colliding power suggested by the fact that over centuries the two had carved out the entire valley.

Nothing, it seemed, of the terrible forces of nature that came in big and small packages. Just the flow, one line into another, as if neither could exist individually.

He thought of the men he had loved, relatively few but with passion. Lionel, the first, a British investment banker whose general uptightness made his sexual openness that much more surprising and powerful, who made great Eggs Benedict and quoted nineteenth-century poets when someone asked how he was feeling—Shelley for happiness, Byron horny, Wordsworth pensive, Tennyson angry. With Lionel, he was sure it would last forever; it ended in two months. Then came Sebastian, the marathon runner, who lacked stamina in bed. George, from Hoboken, who commissioned him to paint a mural of Alexander Graham Bell on the side of his electronics store. And Karl, an acquisitions agent at MOMA, who flattered him by comparing his work to early Van Gogh. All of them sudden, all before he told his family, all gone in a matter of weeks.

Rodney, the marine biologist, lasted almost a year, introduced him to Howard and Rico, insisted on meeting his family, wrestled with Joanne on their living room rug, then promptly cut out for Oregon when a position came open at an Oceanography Institute near Portland. At first he agreed to follow Rodney to the West Coast in a year, then they decided to do the permanent commute, then settled for phone calls, then wrote, then lost touch altogether. "Bad love, Jack," was Rico's thought on the subject, "I never really liked him anyway." "You told me," Howard interjected, "that you would have danced naked for him in a pool of Karo syrup." "What has that got to do with liking him?" Rico retorted, then thoughtfully, "Love was never an option with him, even if you could bounce a quarter to China off his ass."

With Bruce, the chef, things were different, both of them on the rebound, both of them knowing that things were destined to end but willing to ride out events as long as they could. They parted on good terms after two years. Nevertheless, it was Bruce who had called four months earlier and told him without apparent emotion to get tested. Before he received his results, they met for lunch in a downtown café, where he could barely recognize the man he had once loved: trembling hands, gray fedora failing to cover several forehead lesions, green eyes which seemed already dead. They drank espresso, tried to identify the languages spoken by passing tourists, eventually talked about love and fear, held hands, cried a little. When they parted, Bruce said, "Make sure you call me when you find out." But deep down they both knew what the results would be. He had already noticed the first symptoms: weakness, nausea, dizziness. Further conversation would have only put old lovers through unnecessary misery.

After he snapped off another roll of film, he let his hand drag in the river, felt the current hidden there. A chain of men, he thought, whose sins and scents and secrets he could never shake, who had entered him, become him for a time. In a way he pitied the straight men he knew, who would never understand what it was like to be penetrated—sometimes painfully, sometimes pleasurably—but always to feel someone else made part of him if only for a moment. To understand another in a way that required the most intimate and fragile of connections, to receive.

And so he was part of a chain, part of many chains, linking and unlinking to form the story of his life. He thought about his father then, and wondered what that man beyond others had passed on to him, what heredity could account for and what it could not. He remembered how, while Rodney had wrestled with Joanne in their living room, he had confronted his mother in the kitchen, stopped her from slicing chunks of Velveeta onto Triscuits for hors d'oeuvres. How at one point, among the other words that passed between them, he had drawn up short and said, "That's it, isn't it? That's why Dad left. Because he was gay." To which even his mother, even then, had to laugh. "Him?" She shook her head. "He couldn't handle things, is all." She picked up the knife again, held it delicately like a pencil. "Nothing unusual about him. He was a good enough man in theory, I guess. Just never could handle one blessed thing."

• • •

In the middle of the Painted Desert he stopped to write:

The second gunman on the grassy knoll.

He erased and rewrote the line three times before letting it stay. Rico, who was into conspiracies, believed in the second gunman.

Rico had known about the CIA bringing crack into the cities before anyone. The government tests on monkeys and illegal aliens, the missile sites outside Albany, the secret agreements of the pharmaceutical company heads—Rico had all the dirt. Though he had protested with Howard to get gays and lesbians into the local St. Patrick's Day parade, Rico admitted on the side that their plan would never fly. "It's the Pope, man. He's fixed the city elections through 2012. Got that bad Jesus mojo magic. Gets a rise out of anybody."

Nevertheless he had his doubts about conspiracies.

The second gunman: nothing more than a gray photographic blob in a collage of distorted blobs, like clouds which resembled other things but could never be the things themselves. Once he'd attended a rally in Central Park, and his picture had landed on page three of the *Daily News.* Only the reporter had gotten his name wrong in the caption, called him Joe or Jerry. And even though he had told his mother a thousand times who and what he was, she still called to ask, "It's not you, right, Jack? It can't be. The name . . . the name. . . ." Until even he wondered who the person in the photo was, then wondered how deceitful his eyes must be to make him disbelieve himself.

And who was he to worry about the second gunman, anyway? It would be three more years after Kennedy's death until he plummeted into the world. Still, remembering Rico, he figured that maybe the event itself mattered little. What mattered was the way the event lingered in memory, the way it became larger than itself with each retelling. The old myths were the strongest, he supposed, the oldest conspiracies the hardest to shake. The conspiracy of the body against itself, the disease he felt within him, like history, the weight of the past set down on his less-than-Atlas shoulders.

That's how it was at the Grand Canyon. On the south rim, he shut his eyes and tried to imagine himself as the first Spanish soldier to stumble onto the place. Literally, as one story went, a Spanish soldier, half-drunk, crawled through the bushes looking for El Dorado, reached one hand out to find only air, then cleared the brush from his face to stare out over what could have been the end of the world. Brutal, beautiful reality presenting itself in a way that no words could touch. A limit of earth and imagination. Despite the literal grandeur, he kept his eyes closed, breathed in slowly, pushing that myth (of discovery?) to the extremities of his body—feet, hands, hair. Eyes still closed, he drew the camera from its bag and pressed the shutter a dozen times, letting his mind guide the lens. When he looked again, the red walls, red rock had become more than themselves, the air more than absence, the sun more than light. Old myth, first earth. A beginning even as it was an end.

That was the thing about a myth, he decided. Once created, it stayed in the blood, refused to go away. The myths of his time would now be the myths of all time, just as the myths preceding him were part of him in a way he could never fully understand. At the precipice, he stared out and thought maybe this sense—of immersion, of connection—was what he had been seeking. Not just since the disease, but all along.

The sun, noon high, seared its image into the world below, and for some reason he thought of the mural he'd been hired to paint on a hang gliding store in Queens—Daedalus and Icarus—a strange image, he thought, for people in the business of keeping others aloft. The store's owner, nineteen, a CUNY dropout, was emphatic about what he wanted: "Big flames, man. Crash and burn." And so he had painted the picture he remembered from his elementary school reader—Daedalus looking up, surprised—the boy, Icarus, wings ablaze, falling.

But looking over the emptiness of Arizona red, he told himself that he had gotten it all wrong. He imagined Icarus suspended in air, that moment between ascent and fall—feathers, wood, clothes burned away. And Daedalus, his father, beneath him, thinking only of escape. What had possessed the boy to fling himself toward oblivion in this one futile heroic act—suspended before the sun, if only for a moment, its champion? And what had possessed the father to think only of some distant shore, some life of ease, such that he hardly noticed the naked wordless form hurtling past him?

He spread his arms, let the sun beat against him, and almost believed he could fly.

• • •

In his motel room in Flagstaff, he rubbed his eyes then wrote:

Masturbation makes you go blind.

Chains of myth, of blood, of love and desire. They linked the moments of his life together, and linked that life indelibly to the great work of time around it. In the bathroom, he felt his penis move smoothly through his hand, the warm surge of liquid against his palm. Ejaculation did not occur without some pain now—not in his groin, but around his scalp, a pressure behind his eyes wanting to be let out. Opening his fist, he stared at the white gummy mass as if it held some key to his quest. So small, so natural. He lifted his hand to his mouth and rested his tongue lightly against his palm, tasted salt. He had consumed the semen of other men before, but never his own, and thought how odd it was that he chose to do so now, when he was the only one his sperm would not kill. He closed his fist again and considered that strange power, birth and decline perhaps, but more than these the links between him, his parents, his lovers, and all the world that had gone before, combined in his body at invisible levels, embedded in that taste of salt which he only now wanted to understand. Even the disease slowly killing him, that was part of the story, a part of all their stories, the countless billion specks of humanity which commiserated in his blood. Him, here, now—a single strand in the great myths of all time, whether other people wanted to believe it or not.

He turned on the faucet and washed the rest of the semen away with difficulty, having to scrub hard with soap and the fingers of his other hand. Moving into the bedroom, he picked up the phone and thought of Joanne, Rico, Howard, others. But finally he called his mother, never saying exactly where he was.

"Did you find what you were looking for?" she asked at last.

"I'm not sure. Maybe. In a way, I guess."

"Then you'll be coming home?"

A pause. "No, not yet."

She cleared her throat. "Jack, we love you, you know. Your sister and I."

"Yes," he admitted. "I . . . I just wanted you to understand, whatever else you might think, that I'm handling things."

"Of course you are. . . ."

"No. Mother, no. I want you to understand. I'm handling things."

A sound almost like choking came from the receiver. Later he would convince himself that it had been a glitch in the line. "Well, I guess I'll wait for your next phone call, then."

"Yes," he replied, though he might have said more, then hung up.

From the portfolio he took the notebook and turned to the last page, ignoring the numerous blank pages before it. "And they all lived happily ever after," he wrote, then shoved the remaining copies of the living will and as many photos as he could fit in between the pages. He secured the whole thing with several rubber bands, opened the drawer of the bureau, and laid it next to the Gideon's Bible, thinking how the two works fit together somehow—martyrdom, eternity making and unmaking itself, blood and bodies merged to become both more and less than they could be on their own. Outside several children's voices punctuated the grind of a car engine, then disappeared. The sun descended another fraction, sweeping away the rivulets of light sliding past the heavy curtains. His towel dropped off as he lay back in the bed. Running his hands the length of his naked body, he took in the silence like a lover, felt himself pressed down then lifted by the settling air.

The Hand Rebels

So imagine my surprise when I woke to find that my right hand had detached itself at the wrist. My wife and I struggled vainly to put it back, pinning it palm-side up against the table as I searched for seams or slots or even docking clamps which simply were not there. That first night, we locked it in an old typewriter case to prevent its imminent flight.

Soon we discovered, however, that the hand did not want to escape altogether. It merely wished to be free of me. Left to its own devices, it was perfectly content to lounge on the Laura Ashley pillows in the window seat or kick back in the La-Z-Boy, mindlessly flipping through cable channels with the remote. As days passed, I began to chart those things the hand would and would not do. It would not play fetch with the dog, for instance, but would stroke the cat for hours. It would not fix me a sandwich but would prepare a full Greek meal for my wife, including stuffed grape leaves and baklava. It still seemed to enjoy writing and would push a pencil across a legal pad for an entire afternoon. But, being just a hand, it concocted only abstract doodles or the occasional dirty limerick.

I tried to think of ways to coax it back, but since I was right-handed, I realized that the hand had far more to offer me than vice versa. I could keep its nails clean and trimmed, maybe provide transportation, but not much else. Besides, there was my pride to consider. Though clapping proved difficult, I told myself that I could make it as a south-paw. I could scratch myself when necessary, handle a fork, lather up in the shower. I even developed an advanced hunt-and-peck system on the word processor that rejuvenated my writing.

Eventually the hand and I began to function more like roommates than former corporeal partners. The hand sat in on my weekly poker game and took Hank "the Shark" Stromberg for a hundred bucks. It rewired the cable box to get us free HBO. I was finally growing used to the arrangement when I returned one evening to find the hand in bed with my wife. I was torn. After all, it was *my* hand. But then again . . .

"Hand," I said, "this will not do. Either stay away from my wife, or be on your way."

We parted company for good. After its exodus, the hand went on to do a Palmolive commercial, then landed a role in "The Addams Family Reunion Special." It played Rachmaninoff at Lincoln Center and sat next to Madonna on *The Tonight Show.* (This final outrage was enough to make me scream, but since my tongue felt like it too was loosening in my head, I refrained.)

Months later, I learned that the hand had contracted Marty Bristow, my former student, to ghost-write its memoirs. Marty and I got togeth-er for drinks. He looked haggard. "Well, at least the bastard doesn't get out of all the work," Marty said. "It's still got to do the autographs dur-ing the book tour."

"May the hand cramp like a freshman during exam week," I toast-ed. Then, to make us both feel better, I added, "Menial tasks were all it could ever manage, anyway."

The Joke

A priest, a housewife, a chicken, and a bag of chocolate bars are on the bank of a river. They are not sure how they got there but know, collectively, that they are there for the purpose of the joke yet to be told. Uncomfortable as a unit, they take up different positions on the riverbank, waiting for the joke to commence. The sun shines brightly, but a breeze off the river cools the skin. There is a boat nearby: a rowboat, red with white and yellow splashes of paint. The trees on the river's far side bear fruit, though from a distance no one can tell what kind of fruit it is.

• • •

Meanwhile the joker is *not* telling his joke. He sees the characters in his head: an oversexed priest, a voluptuous housewife, a chicken with a Napoleon complex, some chocolate. But he cannot figure out where to go with them. He's had a rough day at work. He's knocked back a few gin and tonics already—less tonic, more gin. He promises himself to try again tomorrow.

• • •

Things grow restless on the riverbank. The priest has missed afternoon confession, and the housewife—whose name is Lila—worries that she forgot to turn off the oven. The chicken, who has been watching the Asian markets and contemplating a major purchase in Chinese poultry feed, curses the malevolent spirit that caused him to leave the coop without his cell phone. Only the bag of candy seems calm. A few feet from the rest of the group, it discovers its own sentience and repeatedly counts the number of chocolate bars it contains. It wonders if the others recognize its new level of consciousness. It resolves to learn how to speak.

• • •

Days pass. The chicken would give his tailfeathers for a single glimpse at the S&P Index. Lila has unbuttoned much of her shirt and tied the bottom in a knot. She describes the riverbank as an adventure that she often longs for but never undertakes. Her husband is a corporate lawyer with a Jaguar and a 7 handicap who gets free T-shirts and gym bags from the tobacco companies he defends. Lila worries about her two sons—fears they will smoke, then hang out with leather-clad women, get tattooed, drop out of school, buy an RV. Her breasts heave slightly. The priest, whose name is Father Ron, watches the heaving breasts. The bag of candy composes, in a difficult Italian meter, an ode in which the river serves as a metaphor for their situation: both movement and stasis. It longs to recite its ode to the others. It pities Lila, and it pities Father Ron, who is now thinking about leather-clad women and an RV known to its neighbors as Lovin' On Wheels.

• • •

The joker cannot get the characters out of his head. At work, he sits in front of a computer screen all day, entering tiny numbers into tiny charts that he has been told are instrumental to corporate success. Sometimes he receives messages from friends, usually of the hey-how-you-doing-isn't-life-boring-as-hell ilk, but sometimes jokes. Funny jokes. Complex jokes. Joke lists. List serves. He is on many lists. He cannot laugh out loud because his boss's secretary might hear him. She knows numbers are not funny. She does not like him because he is somewhat fat, and deep down they both know that fat men are supposed to be funny. In a man, fat without funny is just . . . well, fat. Or Winston Churchill. Or Alfred Hitchcock. He thinks that maybe there is humor in such a realization. His boss's secretary looks up from her *Southern Living*, testing the air. He reverts to numbers. Thinks chicken, candy, housewife, priest.

• • •

The chicken decides that the joke is a hell of his own making. Hubris compels him to believe that, if he can resolve the joke from the inside, he might break out of it. He tries the conventional approach. Why did the chicken cross the road? But here there are no roads, only a river. Somewhere from his youth he remembers a riddle about a farmer with a fox, a goose, and a bag of grain that must all ford a stream in a particular order to prevent any from eating the other. His mind works out variations. In the rowboat, he paddles priest, housewife, and candy across in different permutations—making sure never to leave priest alone with housewife, housewife alone with chocolate. The task is daunting. The oars are insecure. The chicken's muscles ache, and his red comb becomes redder beneath the midsummer sun. The fruit trees on the opposite shore turn out to be lemon trees, ripe with yellow fire. The silence of the lemons makes the chicken uneasy. He thinks of recipes in which he might use their gutted pulp. Lemonade. Lemon chess pie. Lemon drops. Lemon . . . *chicken*. When nothing has changed by dusk, the chicken piles everyone back into the rowboat and returns them to the original shore. He learns to sleep with one eye open, trained on the lemon branches whose shadows reach like dark arms across the water's surface.

• • •

The mind is stuck on itself, the joker decides. It thinks that the world cannot function without it. If a housewife falls in a river but there is no one to hear her scream, no priest to pull her out . . . well, the mind sees the world merely as an extension of such musing. It says, hypothetically, that a chicken walks into a bar. But if a chicken *actually* walked into a bar and made a ranting beeline for the back table where the mind was talking up a couple of Rutgers coeds, it's unlikely that the mind could continue to see the universe as a place of its own invention. In fact, it's likely that the mind would do a screaming tarantella atop the back table until the bartender shooed the chicken out with a broom. This assumes, of course, that the chicken is not a bar regular, and that one of the coeds is not his steady girl Henrietta, and that most of the bar's patrons do not want to buy him a Sam Adams because he is a well-known power broker around town. The mind would have trouble wrapping around such a chicken, but it would be one hell of a joke.

• • •

Meanwhile, Father Ron observes the supple curves of Lila's body. They have now been stranded together for weeks, but she has shown no interest in him. Or, more precisely, she has shown interest in him only as a spiritual confidant—someone with whom she can share all of the problems of her marriage, including her unrequited sexual needs. Father Ron thinks of Job. He wonders if the joke is a test of his spiritual resolve. Thinking along these lines, he notices the chicken, the supple curves of the chicken's body. He tells himself that he is not thinking in a serious way, but in a trapped-on-a-riverbank-with-only-these-questions-to-keep-me-sane way. This is philosophy. He begins to understand why women are called chicks—breasts, thighs, white meat, dark. He starts to dream about chicken. He wonders how egregious some sins might seem before God. The chicken, sensing something amiss, gives up on sleep altogether.

• • •

There is only frustration. Frustration and desire, the joker tells himself, which are really the same thing in the end. He watches the popular men at the bar, whose jokes rise above the smoke and waft into the corner where he sits alone with his domestic beer. How do they begin? Two sisters in Montana must buy a bull for their ranch. An old Jew and a Chinese man are sitting on a park bench. Three hobos eat corn on a train. A doctor's office. A farmer's daughter. A moose. These are items ripe with humor, but when he envisions his joke, he can manage only slight changes: a duck, a rabbi, a librarian, a cherry pie. In the end the joke is futilely the same. Returning from the restroom, he steals a dart from the dartboard and scratches his name into the oak table—then adds some eyes, a nose, and a mouth that resemble a once-famous cartoon cat. His mother always liked his drawings. She hung a few around the house and called him her *artiste*. She said that they would take a trip to France one day, though the closest they ever got was flipping through some travel brochures on Quebec at a rest stop near his cousin's place in Syracuse. At home, after last call at the bar, he will leave two Hungry Man dinners to thaw on the counter of his un-air-conditioned kitchen, then eat them both for breakfast the following morning without cooking them. Later he'll have a bagel at the office, extra cream cheese.

• • •

Egocentrism gets them only so far. At last they decide that the joke is not designed to punish any of them individually. It is merely a random confluence of cosmic forces, the teapot tempest in which they are tossed. They assume that they will be freed eventually but, in the name of order and civilization, agree to rules by which their small society might run. After several halting drafts, they create a constitutional theocracy with the chicken as President, Father Ron as Chancellor, and Lila as Minister of Culture and Good Taste. The bag of chocolate bars, because someone must, becomes the democratic masses. It redoubles its efforts at speech and thinks of the best way for a bag of candy to communicate with the outer world. It could pop its cellophane on a rock and attract throngs of approbative ants. It could melt into symbols on the sand. The First National Assembly is scheduled for a year hence: Father Ron will lead the country in prayer, followed by the chicken's address on the health-care system, then Lila's unveiling of the new Army uniforms made of couch grass and lemon rind. The candy plans a Homeric hymn to commemorate the founding of the state. If it has time, it will fashion some scenery for its performance—perhaps a frieze of the chicken and Father Ron commuting their household gods across the river and onto the riverbank promised in the mystical covenants of their forebears.

• • •

Of course, a joke should be easier to tell. He finally decides that the problem is his mother. When he was a child, she trained him to laugh at misfortune—every accident met with a smile. In this way he learned that pain was comedy. Pratfalls. Pies to the face. A well-placed boot in the groin. He imagines the chicken writhing on the sand, wings to his crotch, moaning "Oh, my nuggets," and he cannot help smiling. His apartment is dark except for the late-night TV. His undershirt rides up his belly where he sticks his hand beneath the elastic of his shorts and cradles his testicles, an unconscious gesture. He sucks an ice cube from his whiskey glass and spits it out the open window, wondering if it might kill a man twelve stories down. Gravity is hilarious, he decides, hefting his paunch with a forearm. The TV audience roars at the host's one-liners. He resolves to get a bigger chin.

• • •

But nothing can help at this point. Long before the National Assembly, friction arises when Father Ron abolishes the institution of marriage and criticizes the chicken's population control plan. They both fear Lila, who has taken to wearing the new army uniform, stockpiling stones, and telling stories of how the Amazons each burned off one breast so as not to impede their bowstrings. An uneasy truce is called. They doff their official vestments, sacrifice the candy bars to a recipe that Lila dubs Couch Grass S'mores, then part ways. As the chicken slips downriver in the rowboat, he dreams of the new society that he will form out of the misfits he finds along his way—characters from bad jokes or other jokes never to be told: one-legged midgets, gay hairdressers, most of Poland. From here on, until his death, he will strive to view himself as a fowl in charge of his own destiny. But even years later, in his tent beneath the mountains—the Sultana's warm body reposed beside him, the drifting incense, and the sound of their many camels spitting in the distance—he will wake with the irrational fear that he is still part of the joke, that he is still working toward some inevitable punchline. There is a spirit at the door of the tent, waiting to sweep in. The chicken stares through the darkness. He sees only the image of his youngest daughter—a red-haired, smoke-eyed beauty who maligns him when she is angry. Silly bird, she chastises. Silly, silly bird.

• • •

Fat man in a little car. Fat man bowling. Fat man in bikini briefs. Fat man doing the cha-cha. Cellulite, he concludes, is the sole of wit. In all honesty, he can do no more with these characters. He detests the chicken and Father Ron. He desires the chocolate bars and Lila. He has grown too close to his material. He's trying too hard. Humor, he knows from somewhere, cannot be forced but must spring from the mind like snakebite. It will come, he assures himself. He just has to wait for it. And when his mind does manage to coil like a rattler, the world will finally see him for the hero that he is. The men will buy him drinks; the women will come home with him, and they will titter in the lavishness of their un-air-conditioned sweat. There will be no calories that laughter cannot melt away. They will love him high and low, the Bobos in their Versace drinking Sea Breezes by the Sound, the Guidos in their leather pants drinking forties down the shore. The elevator door opens onto his boss's secretary who greets him with a sneer. But he exalts in the stale office air, anticipating the day when he is boss and can send her back out because she has not brought a pickle with his egg salad. She, above all, will be forced to acknowledge her treachery, the wanton ignorance of her kind. When the new *him* arrives at the office one day—the joke, the wit, the mind itself—then she will know how wrong she has been. She will see him in the glory of a new light and swear that everywhere she goes they want to be like him: the Bobos, the Guidos, the bosses, the masses. He is his own religion and not the anti-miracle she sees now. Fat man in a cubicle. Fat man at a desk. Fat man who sweats too much. Fat man in off-the-rack pants.

Spelling Lessons

sit on the newly upholstered couch, feeding words out of a dictionary to my eight-year-old daughter, Marianne, who is practicing for the county spelling bee. In the bedroom my wife packs several suitcases—"For when you make it to the state championship," she tells our daughter. My wife, however, has never been *that* much of an optimist.

"Calamity," says Marianne, "c-a-l-a-m-i-t-y." She puts her hands on her hips and whines, "Give me something harder." From the bedroom comes the sound of rattling metal latches, curses, my wife crying softly.

"This is hard enough," I say.

We move through *alienation, disaffected, estranged*. My daughter does not miss a beat. We graduate to *inculpate, perfidious, acrimony*. Marianne's hair is dirty-blond. She is plump for her age, with large round glasses like those of tacky middle-aged women. I pray for contact lenses. She spells *ameliorative* and *palliation* but lingers over *recidivistic*.

The noise from the bedroom subsides, waiting, holding its breath. As Marianne sounds out the word, I suddenly want nothing more than for her to get it right. I want this moment to be my legacy to her, this last bit of certainty.

She stalls according to the methods we have practiced: "Are there alternate pronunciations?" "What is the language of origin?" "Can I have a definition?" But finally there are no more questions to ask. The light of the midday sun rebounds off my wife's Nissan parked in the driveway. The dog and cat both lie in the front yard, and my mind inadvertently assigns labels: mine, yours. I hear my hands folding the dictionary together. Marianne closes her eyes tightly, crosses her fingers, and begins.

Why I Married the Porn Star

She can quote Milton Friedman from memory. She can lock her ankles behind her head.

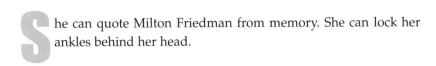

When my mother asks why I married her: I mean, why her and not one of the trillion other girls in the world, why not Lucy Hoffmeiller next door who's the picture of respectability in the neighborhood but would probably get kinky in private, if that's what you're looking for, I reply, I don't know, because I love her. Love, repeats my mother. What do you know about love?

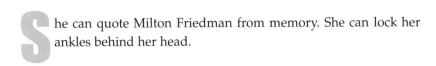

Our first meeting: in the exotic foods section of the local market, reaching for the same kumquats. She was the All-American Girl almost—calves a bit too big, cheekbones too low, hips a touch wide. Later, she would look into my eyes and say that she wanted to take care of me.

• • •

She wears only business suits. Her closet overflows with them. She owns no bustiers, no leather body-suits, no whips, no sexy g-strings, no crotchless panties or fishnet. She is a nineties woman, my wife. She means business.

• • •

We don't have a problem with it, her sister Evelyn claimed when I went to her family's house for our first Christmas together. Sure, maybe at first, but it's only natural then, until you get used to it. Besides, it's nice to have a celebrity around, at least that's what the neighbors say. I'm sure you saw the children waving as you came in. They don't know any details, mind you. We're all Christians here—we just say "movie star" and watch their eyes light up. I mean, even Alice Shockley—the Mrs. *Reverend* Shockley—will tell you in private that the whole thing has really brought the community together. But why do you ask? Do you have a problem with it? Silly me, of course you don't. What could shock a poet? Oh, you better not stand too close to that mistletoe, naughty boy. We're not all as uninhibited as my sister, but none of us balks at tradition.

• • •

Her hair is blond, and her eyes are blue. Her breasts are real.

• • •

We don't have close friends, by and large. Sometimes we hang out with the other porn stars, but I have no idea what to talk about. When they learn I am a poet, they are always intrigued. They say I am in the same business as them, just working a different side of the street. Once a brunette with breasts the size of two challah loaves and breath reeking of Jim Beam plopped down in my lap and told me to write a poem for her. She forced my hand down her blouse and squeezed her fingers around mine. For inspiration, she said. Between her breasts, I could just make out the low-pitched wailing of her heart.

• • •

Sometimes when I want to have sex, my wife says that she has a headache. I ask, Did you have a headache all day? Yes, she replies, but that was business—do you stop working because you have a headache? Somehow I think she misses the point.

• • •

Our city is not one where you would expect pornographers to live. Not to imply anything about the insidious nature of pornographers—this is no conspiracy. It's just odd for a city as conventional as ours. For instance, our street alone boasts four Baptist churches, and just one block over, the entire avenue is devoted to statues of Civil War heroes, dark and imposing in the sense of tradition they inspire. The city loves the war. People here identify themselves by the battles in which their ancestors fought and died. On the Fourth of July, more people stand when the band plays "Dixie" than when it plays "America the Beautiful." The pornographers have ties to the war, as well. One pornographer, who also owns a dry-cleaning business, paid to have the remains of his great-great-great-great uncle moved from South Carolina to the city cemetery so that the old soldier could be buried with his regiment. The pornographer says he loves the South as much as he loves America. His wife is big in the DAR. They have been to our house for drinks, but because of my reluctance to talk politics, we are not close. The pornographer and his wife are not flashy people. When they bow their heads in church, you would not be able to pick them out from the rest of the congregation. My wife is correct, though, when she says that they cannot be upheld as true representatives of the porn industry. They are only representatives of what I choose to see. The other pornographers are nothing like them.

• • •

She has a small tattoo just above her left elbow, a dove with an olive branch in its mouth. She explains, I didn't know it meant anything when I picked it out. I was just a kid. I thought it looked cool.

• • •

From the window by my writing desk, I can see Robert T., the doorman, ushering women from cars at the curb. Robert calls me Mr. Albright and pretends to fuss each year when the Pulitzers are announced and my name does not appear on the list. How is Mrs. Albright? he asks conscientiously when I return from my daily jog. Once, when he thought I could not hear, he looked at my wife and said, Gotta get me some of that. And all I could think was, You can, Robert. Just $19.95. Shipping and handling not included.

• • •

You don't have to worry about my having an affair, my wife says. What do I want with sex? Every woman should be as faithful as me.

• • •

Occasionally she brings home videos to review. She sits before the TV, taking notes on a yellow legal pad in bright red pen. She wears lavender bifocals only at home. The company she works for may let her direct next year, and she asks what I think of this scene or that. Since we have been married, I have seen her in every position imaginable, with a man, a woman, men, women, both. The images no longer excite me. But I can't get over watching her watching herself, sliding her bifocals up the bridge of her nose like a scientist hovering over some new discovery. The voyeur observed. The cerebral irony makes me both horny and ashamed, so much that I have stopped questioning whether the two impulses are truly different at their base. I should take her now, like a beast, bifocals and all. I should write a poem. I am a genius of the perverse, a perverted genius. If only my wife could curve to me like verse—if only verse could hump like a dog.

• • •

But love, she continues. Love is a different story.

• • •

Don't get me wrong, her brother Edmund admitted after several swigs of eggnog, no woman of mine would ever do what she does. But to be honest, I've watched a tape or two. It's like peeking through the bathroom door at them when you're a kid. You got sisters? No? Well, you know what I mean. And hey, if you don't have a problem with it, I say what the hell. It's not like you're married to her or anything. Oh, really? In your pocket? I bet a rock like that set you back a bundle. Oh, no, I won't say anything until you make your move. But listen now, you treat her right. She's my sister. I love her.

• • •

Each year we go to the porn star awards ceremony, and each time I wonder how they determine who wins. Who is acting and how? My wife has won many times. Sometimes while she sleeps, I hold my hand very close to her cheek and wonder if she must act with me. If she acts better than other women.

• • •

So what is love? I insist. Love, she says, is the words around a roll in the sheets—love is the silence between gasps. Face down, I feel her thighs on either side of me, her fists kneading a pain into the small of my back. Leaning close to my ear, she whispers, this is good stuff, are you taking it down? I buck my hips to roll her off. She licks her teeth in serpent ecstasy, and her eyes are shattering mirrors in which I am lost. You should be a poet, I say.

• • •

But love has to be something more. Something deeper.

• • •

I go to the private screenings of her movies. She comes to the private readings of my poems. Being honest, I am a mediocre poet, and the people who come to hear me are mediocre artists in their own right. But we are passionate in our fallibility and cling tightly to ideals which have inspired the truly mediocre for centuries. Mediocre sculptors surreptitiously inspect my wife from across the room. Mediocre photographers cup her jaw in their hands and promise impossible miracles. Mediocre actresses say, if only I had a body like yours.

• • •

I have tried to write her love poems but inevitably fail. Words cannot hold her like fingers. She struggles too much. As to poetry—well, poetry is too imperfect a form for either of our imperfections.

• • •

She has a Psychic Friend—her one vice, she claims—and runs up our Visa bill with 900 number calls. My friend says I have a problem with intimacy, she declares after hanging up—can you believe it, me, intimacy? Intimacy isn't necessarily sex, I reply, it's more like love. If you're suggesting I have a problem with love, she replies, I want to know what accusations like that say about you. Me, I stammer, I don't have a problem with love—with love or anything else. Well, says my wife as she slides another tape into the VCR, neither do I.

• • •

There once was a man from Nantucket. Would you call that a poem?

• • •

But love, she admits, must be more than an exchange of fluids. I know the difference between business and pleasure.

• • •

Once I told her that I could not understand how the men watching her fantasized about her so. It's kind of pathetic, I said, don't you think? To which she replied, I'm not the woman you see. The woman you see is something you've made up, the same way I make myself up when I put on mascara, or a costume, or take any of them off. That's the way reality is. You of all people should know that. I'm no more than a part I have to play, a few words or less, and reality can go to hell.

• • •

Sometimes when we screw, the slats of the bed come loose and the whole frame collapses onto the floor. But by then we are too anxious to stop. We bounce around the mattress like stones loosened from a hill-side. She bites my shoulder. The wet sheet flails my skin and sticks to her long, blond hair. I love you, I scream. Deeper, deeper, my wife replies.

• • •

She has a vaguely heart-shaped mole on the back of her neck where her hairline ends. Right at my brain stem, she likes to say. It's a sign, you see—I had no control over what I chose to do with my life. It was pre-ordained.

• • •

Last night on TV, there was the story of a Norfolk man who caught his wife in bed with her lover, so he killed them both, cut them into a hundred pieces, and piled their remains on a quilt which the women of his wife's family had made as a wedding gift. When questioned, he told police that he only wanted to make her happy, and now the three of them—wife, lover, and quilt—could be together forever. That's a guy who has a problem with love, one cop remarked to the camera.

• • •

Now and then I ask, Am I good in bed? To be honest, she says, I've never really thought about it.

• • •

And then there's Crazy Ethel, the homeless woman who makes her home on the sidewalk opposite our building. She says that she was put under a spell by a man whose love she refused, and it made her teeth fall out. She keeps her teeth in a Ziploc bag in her shopping cart and will show them to passers-by for a quarter. For a dollar, she'll pull out a clump of her own gray hair and promise to bless you over it when the moon is full. She says that God will punish the wicked. I give her a quarter. She eyes me sternly and says, You know who you are. I give her a dollar for good measure. Not that I think I am wicked. But sometimes I wonder if I can be condemned for someone else's sins, if my wife's sins are my own, passed to me through the sweat and saliva of our love. Of course, none of this should matter since God is all-merciful. The young men in starched white collars who stand on the street corner with salvation on their tongues know this. God is love, they declare. But is He a lover? The distinction is essential, inescapable. Or is it? Is God a businessman? What kind of clothes does He wear?

• • •

Shall I compare thee to a summer's day? What does this guy know about love? There is more love in a chipped press-on fingernail scratched down your back than in any stanza this guy could utter.

• • •

She has a small scar on her left foot where the doctors cut away an extra toe after her birth. Sometimes I can still feel it, she says, or maybe I just think I can. It's not like I remember it. Still it would have made me special, and now it's gone. So I miss that toe. Sometimes I think that's what love is, an extra toe. Sometimes I think it wasn't a toe at all, but my heart, and it's out there in a jar of formaldehyde on some doctor's mantle, waiting for me.

• • •

Mediocre poets are a curse, a blinding light switched on only halfway. Lazy mediocre poets are even worse. I should do something definite. Leap from the window beside my desk. Make love to my wife with the camcorder running. Get baptized. Give Crazy Ethel so much money that she plucks herself bald and blesses me for it until the day she dies. Punch Robert T. in the nose. Punch another mediocre poet in the nose. If I had courage to do any of these things, I might figure out what love is, beyond broken mattresses, beyond poetry, beyond bright young men on street corners who drool cleansing fire, beyond a woman whose breasts grow larger as her heart ticks away, beyond my wife, beyond corrective bifocal lenses. Man, woman, men, women. Beyond seeing, almost beyond sense. Together, beyond.

• • •

But when she asks if I have a problem with what she does, I simply wonder whether or not my problems make a difference to her. Only sometimes, she admits turning away, only sometimes.

. . .

And I am not a hero. Several blocks over, the marquee of the adult video arcade advertises a movie starring my wife. In one of the small booths, I slide my quarter into the slot, and the screen buzzes to life. The volume on the machine is broken, so I imagine that my wife speaks poetry as she does what she does, but not one of my poems. I want to see her on the couch with her pad and pen. The light here burns my eyes. From the booth adjoining mine comes a low moan and the sound of a shoe knocking against the wood in steady rhythm. My wife turns and gyrates, ebbs and flows. She is a picture on the screen, a collection of color, a few electric needles, no more. As the camera closes in on her face, her mouth hangs open in expectant silence. I can count her teeth, and my shoulder tingles for the anticipated bite. The man in the next booth screams, I LOVE YOU, and I reach out to touch the screen. Love, I think before my quarter runs out, what do you know about love?

The Suicide

Had she to do it again, she would play music, Debussy or Ravel. And she would choose a nicer hotel, maybe a suite at the Four Seasons or the St. Regis. Somewhere with a picture on the wall—a landscape with people being idle. People happy to be idle.

Doing it again, she would require color, pastel walls to suggest some tone to her life. She would order a ridiculous amount of room service and even request a night on the town. Le Cirque. The Rainbow Room. '21'. She would send her daughters for a fashionable black dress. And she would demand that her husband help her change: lace panties, nylons, pearls. His touch no longer a function of treating her disease. His arms lifting her into the wheelchair like the night they crossed the threshold.

At the restaurant, she would make two waiters carry her down the four steps to the dining area, and she would not flinch when the maitre'd caused a commotion moving tables to fit her in. Let the other diners stare. She would believe she was beautiful.

And later, she would find a way to dance.

Had she to do it again, the doctor who hooked up this infernal contraption would look more like Tom Cruise than Walter Matthau. And he would stand by the bed reassuring her, rather than waiting in the hall with her husband. She would not think about the Schnauzer they put to sleep last year. Or maybe she would think about it and imagine that she was only going to sleep, as well.

She would see the grandkids again, even if they're too young to remember.

Doing it again, she would reserve a room with a fire escape. She would ride in a horse-drawn carriage. She would consume strawberries and lots of booze.

She would ask, just once in her living memory, to be free of pain.

But who is she trying to fool? If she had to do it again, she would not do it. She would ask that someone else bear this torture instead. Yes, God help her, she would. She would remember the time she swallowed kerosene as a child and how her father kept telling her to "hold on" as they raced through the Brooklyn night toward the hospital. She would remember how clean the air smelled and how large the stars looked and how she was not afraid. Not even of death. And she would not "hold on."

She might even refuse to leave the womb.

If she could do it again, she would be the summer wind tugging at her mother's hair. She would be the creaking hinge on the refrigerator door that her father never managed to fix.

She would not press any buttons or see any fluid dripping.

She would not think about what's beneath her skin.

She would not remember her old life. She would promise to enjoy her new one.

She might be more. Or she might be less. But she would not be *this*.

She'd refuse. Somehow.

This much she would.

Clara's PC and
the Second Coming

esus Christ originally spoke through Clara Maples' IBM-compatible thirty years to the day that she had married her husband, Tom, and three years to the day he had run off with the bosomy divorcée who worked at the plumbing supplies depot which he managed. Clara was downloading a recipe for Kung Pao Chicken she'd found while surfing the Web, when suddenly her screen went blank and there appeared the words:

I am the Son of the Living God, the Truth and the Way. I am the Resurrection and the Life. You may call me JC.

Startled, to say the least, Clara punched the Escape button and landed back in the middle of her search page, a list of links confronting her. She clicked on *http://www.sizzlefajitas.com,* spinning her cursor into action. But when the screen came up, this was the only message:

I am the Word made flesh, the New Covenant that is given unto you. I am the Lord of Israel, the Voice from the Whirlwind, the Alpha and the Omega .

She jabbed her thumb against the modem's power switch and shut down her machine, listening as the circuits expired like a breath held in too long. Waiting two minutes exactly before rebooting, she accessed the Net again then headed straight to her mailbox, typing a quick note to Hagyn Sumner, her closest neighbor and Woman's Club car-pool buddy. Five seconds after the message was sent, her computer announced a response. She depressed the "View Mail" button cautiously.

God calling, the message read. *Anybody home?*

Clara ran her fingers over the words on the screen and thought about phoning her older son, Dobie, who sold TVs and stereos at the Circuit City in Glen Allen. But in the end she desisted, afraid of giving him any more ideas about her senility than he already had. For a long time she just sat and watched, rubbing her tongue against her two front teeth, unconsciously reproducing the feeling she got when she drank Coca-Cola too fast. The light from the monitor was an ugly, bad-egg white. In its wake, Clara could make out a cascade of dust swirling by her desk. She rubbed her hands as if to clean them, then pecked out a few characters on the keyboard. Holding her breath, she entered the "Send" command, then exhaled softly as her words spilled into the electronic void.

• • •

"I don't think it's him," Dobie said.

"It could be him," responded Clara.

"Naw," said Dobie, "no way in Hell."

"Don't curse," Clara admonished. "And stop slouching."

Dobie sniffed indignantly but pulled his shoulders upright, making his ample chest and belly appear a little less so. Through his childhood and into high school, Clara had insisted Dobie was merely big-boned, even after her younger son, Martin, told the entire Lee-Davis High cheerleading squad that the name was spelled "Dough-be" because he was so fat. Several years of watching TV fitness gurus had changed Clara's outlook, however. On Dobie's twenty-eighth birthday, she gave him a six-month membership to Weight Watchers and even enrolled herself in a Cooking for Life class at the YMCA. Where before she had made sticky buns and pies, she now kept celery and baby carrots in her icebox and a plastic bag of rice cakes on the table. Dobie liked to slather them up with peanut butter, but Clara had learned to set out only a small dish of Skippy Light when he came to visit, hiding the rest of the jar in the newspaper recycling bin.

"So," continued Dobie, his lips garnished with peanut butter, "how do you know it was him?"

"I told you, we talked." Clara tried to remember all of the afternoon's details. "I couldn't see the harm in a little conversation. It was only polite."

"So what did you say?"

"I said hello."

"Just hello?" Dobie smirked before filling his mouth with another slab of rice cake. "The creator of the universe calls, and you just say hello?"

"Well, what should I have said?"

Dobie rolled his eyes. "I think he's a pervert, Ma. Probably bisexual."

Clara refused to respond.

"Or maybe he's like one of these guys on *Hard Copy*," Dobie speculated. "You know, the kind that marries lonely old ladies then skips town with their money?"

Clara reached over and pulled the dish of peanut butter out of her son's reach. "You're getting to be more like your father every day. You know that?"

"Well, I suppose there are worse things," Dobie replied caustically. He wiped his mouth with the back of his hand then focused on Clara. "All I'm saying is, Ma, don't take this guy too seriously. People have gotten burned by these things."

"I know, Dobie. And I understand you mean well."

Dobie swallowed hard and scratched the back of his head. "I guess I'll take the CPU home with me—poke around the hardware. You won't miss it for a little while, will you?"

Clara wasn't sure if she would miss it or not. "No. You do what you need to."

Dobie watched her lapse into silent thought. "It shouldn't take long," he assured her. "These things are never as complicated as people want to make them. You just have to know what to look for, that's all."

• • •

The machine came back several days later. Dobie had run several pieces of software on it, perused the Web, and given its "innards"—as he called them—a brief once over.

"And no problems?" Clara asked.

"Well, it did levitate off the table and spit fire at me," Dobie said. "But only once."

Clara cleared her throat, pretending not to hear.

"Anyway," Dobie resumed, "no glitches I could find, heavenly or otherwise. Just be careful who you talk to, okay?"

"I will," Clara replied perfunctorily. "And thank you."

Usually Clara took a water aerobics class on weekday mornings, and she never missed *The Price is Right* if she could help it. But after Dobie left, a strange anticipation drew her to the keyboard. I'll just punch into the Net, she told herself as she turned on the monitor. No looking for anybody. Just punch in, and see what happens. She did not have to wait for cyberspace, however. No sooner had she booted up the main drive than the screen flashed three times and the messages began.

Good morning, Clara. I'm glad to see you again.

Clara inspected the screen closely. It appeared to be a regular e-mail board with commands for correspondence at the bottom. She typed a few nonsensical letters to make sure they would appear, deleted them, then began her message in earnest.

Who are you? she typed.

Have you forgotten already? I am the Lord your God, who brought you out of Egypt, out of the land of slavery, etc., etc.

My son says you're a pervert.

Nice boy, that Dobie. But a little on the thick side.

Well . . . are you?

Am I what?

A pervert.

I love all men, if that helps. Also women, children, and creatures great and small.

That's not exactly what I meant.

I know what you meant.

Clara stood up and checked the back of the computer. She didn't know much about the hardware but figured she could identify an extra wire, say, if one were to be found. After tugging on all the cords and checking the electric sockets, she went downstairs to the phone. It offered up the customary dial-tone—no one was sending messages that way. She thought about calling Dobie again but, as before, reconsidered and returned to her machine.

All right. Let's pretend you are who you say. Why don't you do something to prove it. A little rainstorm maybe. Or how about some fish and loaves on my kitchen table?

Sorry, Clara. That's against the rules. You know—thou shalt not put the Lord, thy God, to the test.

Clara snorted skeptically. You expect me to believe God is communicating with me through my computer.

And why not? I figured it might be less threatening to you. You would have preferred a tornado maybe? Or a whale?

An angel would have been nice.

What can I say? The heavenly host has its hands full these days. Besides, you're talking to Jehovah here. It's not like you had to settle.

Well, frankly, I always thought you'd be a bit more impressive. A chariot of fire and all that.

I employ whatever means the occasion warrants. You're only privy to a few of my incarnations.

At least that much Clara believed. She had often wondered how God could be all around her, all the time, like the Bible said. You know, Dobie guessed you might be a giant computer, too, maybe at the FBI or CIA. He's read about those mainframes plotting the downfall of civilization.

And naturally I selected you as my first target .

I confess, I haven't worked out all the details. Maybe I'm some kind of trial run.

Face it, Clara. I am who I am. No less. And no more.

Clara read the words several times. He certainly sounded like God, or at least how she figured God might sound. Of course, he was a bit flippant, but sarcasm was a far sight preferable to fire and brimstone. Besides, if he were the Lord, didn't it stand to reason he'd have a limitless sense of humor to balance out all that righteous anger? The more Clara thought, the more complex the issues became. I should probably go.

Do you really find me less interesting than The Price is Right?

Clara balked. Martin, is that you? Dobie?

We'll talk again soon, Clara.

The monitor returned to normal, the contents of Clara's hard drive staring out at her. She opened a few random files but could find nothing beyond the expected. The digital clock beside her desk sprayed the time across the wall. Eleven in the morning, like it was supposed to be.

Already on the TV, Rod Roddy would be telling some lucky audience member to come on down. Clara's mind was full of invitations as she pushed back her chair, watching pensively until the computer's screen saver kicked in.

• • •

Clara's mother had been a big believer in acts of God. Almost everything that happened—good or bad, large or small—had its direct source in the Creator. As a child, during thunderstorms or after her first cat ran away, such a belief was comforting to Clara. She still remembered her mother's slender figure seated on her bed, the scent of lilac enveloping them, as her mother urged her to sleep with the words of a child's prayer.

But somewhere the ritual had disintegrated. Or more rightly, somewhere Clara had realized it was nothing more to her mother than that, a ritual, disconnected from reality, empty words trying to make sense of a too often empty world. The day Clara's father died in a single car accident, the day Clara got her first period, the day she married Tom, the day her first baby (a girl) died within her—all according to Clara's mother were acts of God. When Tom finally left Clara, her mother was too far gone with Alzheimer's to understand, but Clara had no doubt what she would have said. The same thing she probably said to Saint Peter after Martin and Dobie and several seniors from the church lowered her into a plot at the Westhampton Memorial Park. Acts of God, Clara surmised, there was no getting away from them.

Not that Clara was some kind of pagan. She attended Church on Sunday, as well as some of the Wednesday night suppers, and had faithfully given one hundred dollars to the Lottie Moon campaign each of the last twelve Christmases. But for her, religion would always be a personal matter, an impulse that struck each soul differently, not a bunch of edicts cast down from Heaven like the Hershey's Kisses flung by cheerleaders from homecoming floats every autumn. God did not speak to people out of shrubbery, flaming or otherwise. It was not a question of ability, merely willingness, style. Accordingly, Clara never doubted that God *could* speak to her through her computer, had He a mind to do so. But would He? That was another issue entirely.

"I don't see what's so hard about it. Just pull the plug." Martin's voice shook Clara back to consciousness. He put his hands to this throat and simulated a choking noise until she gave him a look.

They were staring at the blank e-mail screen as it had appeared to Clara earlier in the day. Dobie lay beneath the desk on his back, weeding through a tangle of extension cord, phone line, and connection cable. "Find anything, dough boy?" Martin asked, setting one Air Jordan lightly against Dobie's belly and giving it a shake.

A soft thud emanated from beneath the desk, followed by a thin column of dust, and a volley of coughing. Dobie emerged like a mechanic from under an engine, rubbing his head and glaring at Martin disdainfully. "I hate to admit it, Ma," he began after a few seconds, "but he may be right. Let's connect it to the downstairs jack and see what happens."

Clara was nodding, watching for some life-sign to flash across the vacant screen. She had invited Dobie back for dinner, hoping he would at least pretend to believe her story. Martin just showed up, his Business Systems class at J. Sargeant Reynolds having been canceled. Clara cringed upon his entrance. Bad enough she had to cope with the Savior on her PC, let alone both her sons in the same room for more than an hour. On a scale of mutual antagonism, Martin and Dobie fell somewhere between Abbott/Costello and Cain/Abel. Despite Clara's best efforts at reconciliation—"Who will you boys depend on when I get tossed in a home?" she'd ask—her sons exchanged words mostly out of necessity and, when close, elbowed each other the way they had at ages four and five. Even at her mother's funeral, Clara had been forced to sit between them during the eulogy, and when the time came for them to act as pallbearers, they'd insisted on taking opposite sides of the casket.

They had been surprisingly docile tonight, though, somewhat chagrined by their inability to fix Clara's machine. As before, the e-mail screen popped up no sooner than the computer came on. The boys had taken turns, Dobie first, then Martin, each pecking a key or two, then combinations of keys, then repeatedly mashing the entire keyboard in an attempt to clear the screen away. But to no avail. Even stranger, when Dobie hit the power switch, the computer refused to respond. The white screen just continued to shine like a fixed, pupilless eye. As

Clara and Dobie watched, Martin wrapped his hand around the main power cord where it connected to the wall socket. "Just one good yank," he repeated.

A moment later the plug was in his grip, swaying like a snake under a charmer's spell. Dobie looked from the socket to the screen. He nudged Clara's shoulder, as if she needed nudging. The monitor still glowed.

"What the hell?" Dobie began, running his palm over the glass front, then rapping it with his knuckles. He dropped to a crouch and started to churn computer wire through his legs like a retriever. When he stood up again, the snarl of cords in his hands resembled spaghetti.

Martin continued to stare at the plug, mesmerized. "Jesus Christ," he whispered.

A whir of machinery, a flash of light, and black pixels arranged themselves on the screen. *Yes?*

In the ensuing silence, Clara regarded her sons meaningfully, the desired "I told you so" caught somewhere between her teeth and kidneys. Dobie reached out to touch the machine like an ape from the beginning of *2001*. He jerked back upon first contact, then laid his hand delicately across the computer's top, stroking it like he would a newborn baby or a pit bull.

Well, the message read, *type something.*

Dobie extended both index fingers and plucked out a line. We are you?

Haven't we been through this already?

Dobie frowned. We are peaceful beings. We mean you no harm.

What am I? A Klingon? I'm not here to take over the planet. I already have dibs. Remember?

Martin chuckled, "Don't make him angry, Dough boy. He might turn you into a water buffalo. Then again, that might be a step up."

"It isn't God," Dobie snapped, ignoring the insult. "I mean, God doesn't just show up in people's IBM's. At least not in ours."

And why not? You think the wife of a Jewish carpenter is any different? Or an Arab camel driver? There was a pause as the cursor spun several times. *You need to have faith, Dobie. And stop slouching.*

"Wha—?" Dobie's bottom lip trembled slightly, a dewdrop of saliva pirouetting to the carpet. "You can hear us?"

And then some. They don't call me omniscient for nothing.

Martin had already hit the floor, running his hand under the day bed and along the desk, searching for a bug. Dobie scanned the ceiling as he spoke. "No, it's not true. The real God doesn't come to people like this any more."

What do you mean? How about Gandhi, King, Mother Teresa—

"That's different."

—Wiesel, Sakharov, Ollie North—

"Ollie North?"

Just making sure you were still with me. Hey, Martin voted for the guy.

"You voted for North?" Dobie yelled at his brother, who was halfway through an inspection of the bookcase.

"What's it to you?" Martin replied.

"You really *are* an idiot, aren't you?"

"Go to hell."

"Boys," said Clara.

Look, nobody goes to hell without my say-so.

"Oh, this is rich," ranted Martin, stomping back across the room. "You know, you speak pretty good English for a two-thousand year-old Jew."

Oyvez, you tink mebbe I oughtta talk like dis. I created the universe. Noah Webster I think I can handle.

Martin flared his nostrils but kept quiet. When Dobie poked him and motioned around the room inquisitively, he shook his head, frowning. Clara gave the high sign for them to adjourn to the hall. "Well, what do you think?" she asked seconds later, shutting the door to keep the computer from their line of vision.

"I think we need help," Martin said. "God or not."

Dobie relinquished his breath like a balloon let loose. "I know a couple of guys at Radio Shack," he said.

"Actually," Martin replied, eyes narrowing, "I was thinking of someone a little more potent." He bit his lip in an expression of grim resolve.

• • •

The Reverend Jimmie John Cavanaugh and his entourage arrived two days later, packed into a blue and white love bus with the words

"God's Battalion" spray-painted on the side. Jimmie John wore a white tuxedo jacket and slacks with Pat Boone shoes and matching Beatitudes bow tie and cummerbund. He shook hands with Martin in the driveway then crossed himself before proceeding up Clara's porch and into the parlor. The entourage tagged along closely—Phil, a pale rake of a man with weasel eyes and pop-bottle spectacles that made his retinas look even smaller; Lula and Lola, twin sisters dressed in white to match Jimmie John, who between them weighed as much as the love bus; and a waist-high, severe-looking Vietnamese boy referred to by all as Smiley. Phil carried a video camera and followed Jimmie John assiduously, aiming the camera per the Reverend's instructions, taking extended shots of a chair, a light, a wall. Lula and Lola stayed on the porch singing "Christ the Lord Is Risen Today" until Jimmie John beckoned them in, while Smiley pulled various religious accouterments from the van and spread them across the lawn: a cross made of badly stained two-by-fours, a menorah with several pink and green candles, a pile of white bedsheets. Clara pulled aside a curtain and stared up and down the street, thankful she could see none of her neighbors. Behind her, Dobie and Martin argued.

"This is the best you could do?" Dobie said.

"Hey, J. J.'s all right. Besides, he was the only one who'd come on short notice, and he's working for nothing."

Dobie grunted as he straightened an Ansel Adams print which had been knocked askew at Lula and Lola's passing. "So where'd you meet him, anyway?"

"In a bar in Hampton Roads," Martin answered. "When I was down for army reserve training. Apparently he runs a church for military personnel."

"He looks like a mortician on prozac to me."

Martin made a gesture Clara couldn't see. He smiled when he caught her looking. "Don't worry, Mom. You're in good hands."

"Maybe," Dobie muttered ominously, to which Clara silently agreed.

The Reverend Jimmie John came back through the parlor and into the living room, Phil trailing a few steps behind him. He shook hands with Martin again, then Clara, and laughingly slapped Dobie on the shoulders. Phil got close-ups of the whole scene like a reporter following a candidate on the campaign trail.

"I've inspected the premises," Jimmie John began, "and can't say as I find anything extraordinary—bleeding walls, pillars of salt, and such. But appearances can be deceiving. You can't be too careful when dealing with such claims."

"So you've done this before?" Clara ventured.

"Done this before?" Jimmie John seemed genuinely surprised. "I should say I have."

"Tell them about Georgia, J. J.," Martin offered.

"I hate to toot my own tuba," said the Reverend.

"Aww, go on."

"Well, if you insist." He leaned close to Clara as though revealing a secret. "You know that little old lady in Conyers who received the Word of the Madonna? I confirmed it." Phil pushed between the two of them for a better camera angle. Jimmie John continued. "And the sighting of the Holy Supper on that silo in Farmville—mine, as well."

"What," Dobie muttered, "no walking on water yet?"

"Give me time, son." Jimmie John positively glowed. "Give me time."

"It's not that we doubted your credentials," Clara resumed, stepping in quickly to cut off Dobie's response. "But you might find this case a little different."

"They're all a little different. That's what makes this job a challenge."

Clara nodded. "I suppose so. But may I at least show you upstairs, perhaps turn on the computer for you?"

"Thank you, no. Your son has apprised me of the situation, and as a rule I feel it's best to go these things alone. No outside influences, you understand." Jimmie John rubbed his hands in anticipation. "If you could just direct me to the device in question . . ."

"Left at the top of the stairs, last door on your right. The computer's in the far corner."

Jimmie John nodded. "All right, then, let's do God's work." With a flourish he stepped past Phil into the parlor, where Lula and Lola waited. "Onward, Christian Soldiers" was struck up, and the four of them launched their way upstairs.

For the first few minutes, Clara, Dobie, and Martin could hear only muffled voices, then some knocking on the walls, then muffled voices again. Smiley entered the parlor, frowned at them in the living room, then proceeded upstairs. He came back down seconds later and out the front door. The voices never stopped. Clara looked questioningly at Martin, who gave her a self-satisfied grin. Smiley returned with the cross made of two-by-fours, thumping it against each step on his way to the room, and as he opened the door, Lula and Lola burst into the first few bars of the Halleluiah chorus. The door shut quickly, Lula and Lola began to climb Jacob's Ladder, and above it all the Reverend Jimmie John prayed, sometimes in a dull monotone, other times in a boisterous howl, both of them equally incoherent.

Fifteen minutes passed, then a half-hour, an hour. Smiley made several trips up and down the stairs, bringing with him the menorah, two gallon jugs of spring water, and a four-foot cardboard cutout of the angel Gabriel. Lula and Lola ran through a litany of spirituals, the Doxology and the Gloria Patri twice, and what sounded like the theme to "Godspell." This was followed by more praying and some stomping, then yelling, louder and louder. Suddenly the table lamp next to Clara dimmed, and there came a sound like some villain getting vaporized in a science-fiction movie. They heard the door open upstairs, and the Reverend Jimmie John shouted, the words that streamed from his mouth anything but holy. He hit the downstairs at a dead sprint, stumbling into the living room, eyes wide, cheeks red and pasty, his collar jerked open and the Beatitudes bow tie nowhere to be seen. "I have never in all my born days," he stammered. "That thing—it ain't no work of God. It's a demon."

Behind him, Phil and Lula and Lola churned down the steps, carrying the camera, the cross, and several other items. Smiley and the angel Gabriel brought up the rear. Jimmie John was shaking his finger at Clara. "I don't know how you found out those things," he said. "And I don't know how you got them on your computer. But I'll tell you this, if you ever repeat them to another living soul, I'll sue you for libel and take every cent you've got."

Clara stared in amazement. "Reverend, I'm sure I don't understand."

They could hear Phil revving the love bus outside. Jimmie John smiled a half-crazy smile. "Oh, you understand all right. Don't think I'm not gonna put the word out on you. There won't be an evangelist within three countries that'll come ten miles from this place. I've got your number, lady. Oh, yes I do."

"J. J., this is crazy," Martin said. "If you'll just give us a minute—."

"And one of my own flock, too," Jimmie John interrupted. "Judas in the garden." His voice echoed off the ceiling.

"Now wait a damn minute," Martin continued. But before he could finish, the Reverend whirled and stalked out the door. They listened as the love bus spun gravel, then screeched like a baby condor when it hit the pavement of the street. Martin stared at the open door. "Well—shit," he managed.

Dobie was nodding, breathing heavily through his nose. "What does he know anyway? We don't need him. We can play this thing however we please. We'll put an ad in the paper." His eyes lit up. "We'll put ads in all the papers. Come and see God's computer, we'll say. We can charge admission, five bucks at the door, fifteen if you want God to answer some personal question. We don't need the Reverend Jimmie John. We'll do just fine."

"You may have something," Martin agreed, nodding thoughtfully before crossing over to lay a hand on Dobie's shoulder. "We can sell concessions, maybe even souvenirs. 'My Mom and Dad spoke to Jesus, but all I got was this lousy T-shirt.' How does that grab you?"

Clara watched the two of them, faces bright, and wondered why after so many years it was only this fiasco which could bring them together. "No," she said softly when they paused. "No."

"What do you mean no, Ma," Dobie asked. "This is it. This is our chance."

"I won't have it," Clara replied. "God or not, that thing upstairs was meant specially for us. I won't exploit it. And I won't exploit innocent frightened people, either. I won't be another Jimmie John, you understand?"

Only when she stopped did she realize how shrill, almost desperate, she sounded. Dobie and Martin, their plans deflated, just stared. "So—what do you want us to do?" Martin finally asked.

"Go home."

"Ma?" Dobie whispered.

Clara looked straight at them and, though she felt ready to cry, managed a smile. "Go home, boys. I'll figure out something. I'll call you."

The three of them stared at each other a few moments longer. Then Martin turned toward the door, pulling Dobie by the elbow. Clara watched through the window as both their cars disappeared down the street.

• • •

Clara had lived near Richmond her entire life and never much wanted to leave. Of course, she had never anticipated certain things. That her husband would walk out after thirty years of marriage, for one. That when he was gone, she would realize how little of the world she had experienced. That she would raise two sons into the same mediocrity in which she had trapped herself. And that one day a few seemingly insignificant words on her computer would offer her a new beginning, if only she were willing to accept it. Did it really matter whether the messages came from God or not? Clara wasn't so sure, for the words had reminded her of the possibility of change, even now. Hope springs eternal, wasn't that the saying? And she was only fifty-four—no spring chicken, but hardly a relic either. Who was to say, as Tom had said for so long, what she should and shouldn't do?

She remembered a bus ride she had taken as a teenager, a school trip from Mechanicsville, her home, to the monuments of Washington D.C., the closest she had ever been to real history and most likely would ever come. She had sat next to Connie Reynolds on the drive up, but, returning, Connie had swapped places to be next to Jack Philips, star tight end. Clara had ridden next to Winston Garish, star of the Latin Club. Not that Winston was a poor catch. He was courteous and friendly enough, clean-cut like the military boys Clara had seen at the fairgrounds, and intelligent. He told Clara how he was headed to Wake Forest the next year and how he planned to be in Europe as soon as he graduated college. "Not for anything special," he said, "just to go once before my life really starts." Clara said it must be nice to have such dreams, though she hardly knew if she meant it. To her, Europe was little more than a yellowing map on the wall of Mr. Kern's history class. And, besides, didn't travel require money, and hadn't she already pledged herself to the secretary's job that Mrs. Boone, the typing instructor, had found for her? Winston made Europe sound lovely and exotic, castles along the Rhine, the canals of Venice—and everybody knew about the French, he said, giving her a nudge. Clara didn't know doodly-squat about the French, but she nudged Winston back, and told him he'd do well at Wake, and hoped he wouldn't forget all the homebodies like her when he was off gallivanting in Greece or Austria or wherever it was.

Five years later, she received word from him on a postcard of the Champs Elysées. He said he could book her passage on the next plane over, and they could view the windmills of Holland and the ruins of Rome together. It would be just like some old movie, he said. But Clara was already seeing Tom, and things were turning serious, and she simply couldn't give up her job now that Mrs. Godwin had taken maternity leave and placed her in charge of the secretarial pool. She sent Winston a telegram, eighteen words for which she paid two dollars and fifty-five cents, closing, it seemed to her, several chapters of her life in a single turn.

Surprisingly she hadn't thought of Winston or what it would have been like to say yes to him for years. Despite its mundanity, her life never allowed pause for things like dreaming or reflection. Yet now, with God housed in the spare bedroom one floor up, she couldn't help but realize how random life really was and how beyond her control it had always been. That's why she had given up Winston and dreams of Europe, she told herself—for normalcy, to have the kind of ordered life that everyone from her mother to her gynecologist had taught her to want. So where was the order now? In a way, she hoped, even prayed, that whatever had taken possession of her computer was not the Almighty. For even though she was grateful for the second chance occasioned by his arrival, she was also angry that he had not appeared to her sooner, headed off her mistakes, let her know up-front the rules of the universe, namely, that the cosmos didn't give a tinker's damn what happened to her. Now here was God, or the next best thing, with his message of all being well again. And maybe Clara did have time to act on that knowledge, but maybe she didn't either, and it was this second possibility that both scared and enraged her in ways she'd long assumed impossible.

After Dobie and Martin's departure, she moved upstairs to assess the damage caused by Jimmie John's visit. The room was surprisingly clean, the only trash being the empty gallon jugs, though what Jimmie John had done with the water they contained was a mystery to her. She went to the computer and waited for something to happen, which it did, moments later.

I don't think you'll make Jimmie John's Christmas card list.

"I would ask what you said," Clara countered. "But I have a feeling the less I know, the better."

Perhaps. But men like Jimmie John—they serve their purpose, too.

"You're not banishing him to hell, then?"

I hate to tell you this, Clara, but there is no hell. It was a ruse.

"You're joking."

Not about this. What did you think I meant by all that prodigal son business? Redemption is always there, to the very end, even after. You just have to take it.

"But not everyone does."

No, not everyone. A good number, though. And you'll find that as eternity proceeds, people come around.

"I see."

You're not here to talk about Jimmie John, however.

Clara swallowed hard. "No, I'm not."

What, then? I've been known to offer an answer or two in my day.

Clara thought a long time before she spoke. "Why me?" she finally said.

Why not? Maybe I just want to keep the word spread, and this is my way of doing it.

"Yes, but why *me*? You could have picked anybody."

There was a short pause before the answer. *Then I ask again, why not you? Why someone else instead?*

"You're being evasive."

You don't want me to pull rank, do you? Who art thou to question the Lord and all."

Clara tried to remember where the words came from but could not. "I have a feeling it's because you're lonely," she continued.

Pardon?

"You heard me—lonely. I'll be honest. I don't know if you're God or not. But let's say you are. I've often wondered why you'd want to make the world, and the best I can figure is that you're lonely in your own way. Humans are a mess, you must admit. You could zap us into submission anytime you choose, but that's not what you want, a bunch of craven mice. You need people to have free will so there can be something outside of you, if that's possible. You need somebody to talk to, some sense of otherness—maybe not exactly the way we feel it, but close enough. I figure that's why you selected me, because I was lonely, too."

Is that so? Well, I can't say whether you're right or wrong, though I'm given to understand I work in mysterious ways. If it's any help, Clara, creating the universe was nothing compared to creating myself.

"That much I believe," Clara admitted. "I guess my only question now is whether you are who you say or not?"

But does that even matter? If it's just loneliness binding us together, does it matter whether I am God, or another human being, or a computer, or just some errant thought drifting through the universe?

"Maybe not. Except as it affects what I do now."

That's always the question, isn't it? Perhaps the fact that you are committed to doing something *is enough in itself.*

"Seems a little vague to me."

Even so—.

In Clara's mind, the events of the past few hours and days blended back through the preceding years. She touched the screen carefully. "I won't be seeing you again, will I?"

No. A pause. At least not here.

"It's just as well. Who knows what scheme Jimmie John's concocting?"

He's no longer a threat. Never was, really.

"I know. I'm just saying."

Clara, don't worry about Martin and Dobie. They'll be fine. I have my eye on them.

"I know that, too."

Good-bye, Clara.

As the light of the monitor folded in on itself, Clara's hand dropped away. "Good-bye," she echoed. For the first time in days, though it seemed much longer, the screen subsided to black. Clara felt behind the monitor, back where the cables bunched and mingled, but they weren't even warm.

• • •

At first her thoughts turned to Winston Garish and Europe. She had saved some money, and there would be no problem getting tickets. Several times Dobie had shown her how to make reservations through the computer network service to which he subscribed. She could be in

London in a week, Rome in a month—and from there, who knew? But for some reason, the idea of Europe failed to satisfy her. Travel would make her no younger, no less alone. She had a life to live now, in the present. To try to go back and redeem every mistake she had made—well, *she* had made them, and they would be a part of her forever. Besides, given their variety, she doubted she would have enough space in several lifetimes to compensate for them all.

Then she turned to the Bible, reading the important passages, skipping Deuteronomy and the "who begat whoms." She watched TV preachers and probed the inspirational sections at local bookstores. She fasted for the better part of one Sunday until Dobie told her she looked peaked, when she took a V-8 and a hard-boiled egg. She prayed.

And finally she went back to her computer, logging onto the Internet and setting up her own site, *http://www.godhelpshere.com,* printing this message along with her address on the screen: "I have seen the Lord. He is well. I am willing to talk to anyone who wishes it. Clara."

The first few days brought the expected responses.

Monday. I saw Jerry Garcia at a Phish concert. Let's get together and jam sometime. Casey Jones.

Tuesday. SWM, nonsmoking, Christian, 41. Seeks born-again SWF, 19–41, who likes hiking, cats, and Amy Grant. Interested in exclusive relationship, perhaps intimacy. No smokers or atheists need apply. Write Charles at above address.

Wednesday. Crazey bitch . . . weenel done her mos everthing ;;Crhist suks!!!!!!!!

But after several weeks, Clara's incoming mail turned up this query. Did you mean what you said?—Denise

Clara copied down the address and wrote back that night. I did. Though it sounds absurd, here is what happened. And she told the story, from JC's first appearance to his last, about Martin and Dobie, about the Reverend Jimmie John, about the doubts she entertained at first, and still did. She said that God was lonely, and then told how Tom had left her three years earlier, and how she was lonely, too. She even told about Winston Garish and her chance to go to Europe, but added that maybe talking to God was better, even if it turned out not to be God in the end. She did not interpret things, at least so far as she could help it, but simply recounted the events before sending her message along.

Denise wrote back the next day.

Dear Clara,

Thank you for your story. I don't know how true it is, but it is a good story and may mean something to me, though I don't yet know. As best I can tell, you are either the craziest person in the world or the sanest. I am the same way. I have a story, also.

It's been several months since I've really spoken to someone—at length, I mean. My husband, Garrett, is a good and devoted man, and he is willing to listen, but for some reason there are things I cannot tell him. I look in his eyes and see pain, and I don't know if it is pain for me, or for himself, or for both of us, only that to speak is to cut deeper rather than to heal. Perhaps that's why I'm writing you, a stranger, because you may not be such a stranger, after all. Maybe you are the listener I've been looking for. Even if not, you are many miles away and can only hurt me so much.

We moved here—San Diego—from very near where you are now. Being in the navy, Garrett goes where he is ordered, as do I after a fashion. We had a baby—a boy, Joshua, who died. Sudden Infant Death Syndrome, the doctor said. We thought about the things we might have done or not done, been more careful to make him sleep on his back and the like, but the doctor said it was not our fault. Garrett wants to have another child when I am ready, but I can't say when I will be, if ever. Sometimes I think people are allotted only a certain amount of love to give and that my share died forever in that crib with Josh. I feel almost idiotic telling you this, embarrassed. What kind of mother must I have been, you're probably thinking. So I'll tell you what I've decided. I wasn't a good mother, and I wasn't a bad one. I was a brief mother, and I can't help but feel that, in being so, I lost more than I'll ever regain.

Why am I telling you this? I don't know. My people are Presbyterians, never what you would call devout, and it's only in the thick of this mess that I've started thinking of God again. And not in good ways, mind you. I wonder most if there's a plan to it all. I know I sound like a newspaper advice column, but the question won't go away. Some days I ask myself how a merciful God could do something like this both to me and to an innocent child. Other days I answer myself, and I say either that God is not merciful and loving, as I once believed, but random and vindictive and maybe even evil, or that He does not exist at all, and I don't have a strand of hope.

That's what I need from you, I suppose: hope. I need to know that God, or something, is out there and that the reasons may be beyond me but are there also. You said that God was lonely. I don't want to be alone. I want to look at the sky and see more than sky. I want to believe this stale world is actually alive. But I also want my son back, and that will never happen. And if that never happens, maybe nothing else will either. And maybe I am foolish and have always been.

I am sorry. Thank you for listening. If you don't write back, I'll understand.
—Denise

To her surprise, Clara's first reaction was skepticism, for it occurred to her that she had never seen Denise before, and as Dobie said, you never knew who was writing what on the Internet and why. But by the same token, she had never seen Europe, either, yet had no doubt it was there. In fact, she began to think that Denise—well, Denise and people like her—were the whole reason she had been contacted in the first place. "Maybe what I found," she told Martin later on, "wasn't God but faith, which covers a lot more ground and is probably more useful in the end." There was still the matter of JC's identity, of course, and Clara had been thinking about the Internet—that electronic world where by the stroke of a finger in her spare bedroom she could touch San Diego or Paris or wherever. Didn't it stand to reason, despite the logical objections, that something that vast had to possess a mind of its own, in a manner of speaking, and a moral sense and emotions which didn't mind reaching out now and again?

Finally, however, she dismissed those mysteries she could not solve. For no matter the truth about God, she had her story, and it wasn't so much the facts of that story as the fact of story itself in which she believed. The word is truth, Clara remembered, and the truth shall set you free. She wrote back to Denise, and they started to correspond on a more regular basis. But every time she punched the button that would rocket her words along wires from one coast to the other, she recalled with great clarity the sentiment with which she had begun her second letter to San Diego. She had heard the words many times before, even said them herself, but never with quite the sense in which she now understood them.

Denise, she wrote, do not worry. You are never alone.

Fish Story

After the trout that contained the soul of my mother, I hooked this carp that must have been Dad. So I said to him, "How's tricks, Dad? You know, I've got Mom in the ice chest"—a statement which, in my opinion, deserved more than the blank stare he gave me. Then again, I doubt he ever expected to run into me on the Susquehanna River, and I felt sorry for him in a way, since he was Baptist and didn't plan on being reincarnated, especially not as a mud-sucking bottom feeder.

So I tossed him into the ice chest with Mom and added water to make them comfortable, then shut the lid so they could be alone. And around midday I fell asleep and had this dream where I pulled them out of the ice chest and fileted them for lunch. I felt so bad when I awoke that I considered throwing myself into the river, but just then I snagged this perch with spectacles and a German accent, who told me that sometimes a trout is just a trout. Still I was hungry, so I ate the perch, and was satisfied. I gave the perch's spectacles to Dad, and he slapped his lips together several times in appreciation. Then I threw both parents back, and they swam off in different directions, which made sense, because before Dad got run over by that back hoe in real life there had been much speculation about his ties to the girl with the lazy eye who sold mulch at the annual convention in Johnstown.

Nonetheless, you see how I couldn't catch more fish—since they were actually souls of the departed—which is why I stopped at Herman's Grub Shack and had a beer while I waited for the ribs to cook, and told this story to Loretta the waitress, who thought I was noble and gave me a peck on both cheeks, which explains the lipstick. And that's why you, my wife, have nothing to worry about.

But what does it all mean, you ask? Beats me. Maybe something about love. I guess I should have asked Mom and Dad—and I *will* if I see them again. But I figure they'll have to be cold and slippery a good while before they get any answers. I mean, fish have been rooting around in the muck for centuries, yet even the smartest ones seem miles away from understanding entanglements of the heart.

Love in a Straight Line

69. If there be a pure love, free from taint of other passions, it is hidden so deep in our hearts that we are not aware of it ourselves.

136. Some there are who would never have been in love, had they never learned the word.

—*La Rochefoucauld*, Maxims

ike a perplexed Schnauzer, Carl Mullen watched from his driveway as the woman from the Hudson Valley Art Historical Society perused his detached garage. She had called a week earlier to let him know she was coming, but he'd assumed it was a prank, some of the high school kids on spring break, right until her Cadillac had appeared next to his rhododendrons. His eyes tracked her from weed whacker to fertilizer to the stand of rakes in a far corner, and he found himself wishing that he'd chosen a nicer outfit for the occasion. Tuesday was his customary day off from the toll plaza on the Tappan Zee Bridge, and he liked to maximize his relaxation time. He pulled his T-shirt away from his chest and read the front—*Ashtabula Arts Fest* in faded red letters—a present from his ex-wife Joanne more than ten years earlier. He was still trying to figure out how to look casual covering the various stains when Marilyn Hartsworn returned from the rear of the garage.

"It's just as I imagined," she announced, stepping into the sunlight. Carl's eyes darted among the spots of loose stucco, then down to the two-foot fracture where his basketball goal had met the wall during a storm the previous summer.

"So this Georg Von Hersel," he resumed tentatively.

"The Master of the Straight Line."

"Pardon?"

"That's what they called him."

"Oh," Carl squinted as he pretended to file the information away. "You're sure he lived in my garage?"

"For a few months, yes. In 1948."

Carl had bought the house outside Cold Spring in the early eighties, and no one had mentioned Von Hersel. Still, with the amount of history that choked the lower Hudson Valley, he figured anything was possible. "And he was famous?"

"Some critics think he was as revolutionary as Pollock or Franz Kline."

Her voice betrayed a note of self-satisfaction that put Carl off for a second then drew him more forcefully to her. "My ex-wife knew something about artists. She could tell you their gimmicks."

"They're not gimmicks," Marilyn prompted. "They're aesthetic principles." Her sandy brown hair had been pulled into a bun, and her blue eyes, which rarely blinked, were set over a nose that came to a point like an awl. Even in the April humidity, beneath her khaki business suit and makeup, she did not seem to sweat. She was a little over forty, Carl guessed. He nodded sheepishly as she motioned him back toward the garage. "We'd have to renovate before the tours," she said. "At the Society's expense, of course."

"And people will pay to come in?"

Marilyn shrugged. "We do good advertising. We list with the AARP."

Carl tried to imagine it: busloads of tourist brochures and orthopedic shoes bubbling up his driveway for their brush with art celebrity. Still, he was a quarter-mile from his nearest neighbor, so no one would be disturbed. "Go out with me," he blurted.

"I'm sorry?"

It was not the opening line that he'd intended, but he was stuck with it. "Go out with me," he repeated, "and I'll sign the agreement today."

Love in a Straight Line

In the moment that Marilyn's nose turned decidedly upward, before she let her shoulders relax, Carl knew that he desired her. He wished even more fervently that he had come to the door in something better than his T-shirt—a polo with a sweater tied around his neck, perhaps, or a smoking jacket. It occurred to him that he had no idea where Ashtabula was, but standing in front of Marilyn Hartsworn, he longed to know things that might impress her. If she asked, he decided that he would tell her Ashtabula was in Indiana, a small place through which he and Joanne had once traveled on their way to Chicago, even though he had never been west of Buffalo.

"When?" Marilyn replied suddenly.

"Tonight," Carl offered, surprised. Then not wanting to appear desperate, "Tomorrow?"

Marilyn drew a pen and several forms from the bottom of her portfolio, passing them to him. "I'll be here tomorrow at 7:00. You pick the place. Nothing too fancy."

• • •

Two weeks and several dates later, Marilyn sent her contractor to Carl's door. Mike Rocket was middle-aged and balding, with three gold studs in one ear and shorts a size too small. His right shoulder sported a horse-head tattoo, faded and big-eyed, that made Carl feel as though Mike were watching him even when he wasn't. In five minutes of conversation, Mike revealed that he had grown up on Cape Cod, quit drinking without the help of a twelve-step program, and retired from twenty-seven years in the Coast Guard after deciding that he had always hated the ocean. Carl figured he was gay, except that Mike made obscene references to Marilyn's breasts. "I played Legion ball with a kid whose mother had a rack like that."

"I don't like baseball," Carl said.

Mike seemed unfazed. "So you a member of the Arts Society?"

"They just need my garage."

"More power to you." He reached back to extricate a wad of shorts that had wedged into his butt. The horse head stared at Carl coolly. "People up here," Mike continued, "are always doing work. It's like they piss nickels or something." He motioned to the driveway. "Hang

- 135 -

around a second, and I'll give you a spot diagnosis."

As the contractor headed toward the garage, Carl sat on the porch, deciding what to think of him. Marilyn had never worked with Mike before, though she had repeated the phrase "highly recommended" several times when describing her decision to hire him. He was a little coarse for Carl's taste, but he was sincere. And honesty, Carl had to admit, was a dying art.

It was in this spirit of honesy that Carl had tried to be candid with Marilyn and revealed—over pricier dinners than he was accustomed to eating—everything about himself that wouldn't absolutely scare her off. He told her the story of his dropping out of Southern Connecticut State and starting with the Transit Authority, working his way up to manager on the Tappan Zee Bridge. And the story of how he had met Joanne at a party in Greenwich when she was twenty-one years old and he was thirty-two—the pregnancy and the civil ceremony that only Joanne's mother flew in from Wisconsin to attend. He told her about Joanne's ambition to become an artist, about the loom still in his basement, and the way he had spent many nights sleeping alone because of the sudden inspirations that would hit her. And once, at a German restaurant outside Fishkill, he even told her about how, near the end, he had requested several months off from work to drive Joanne to shows around the region in an attempt to make things right between them again. "It didn't take," he concluded.

Marilyn's fork hovered a few inches above dessert, a flat mixture of peach and pastry. "So your child lives with Joanne now?"

Carl shook his head. "Joanne miscarried late. They couldn't save the baby."

"Oh, Carl, I'm sorry."

He shrugged. "It was a long time ago. Fifteen years this October."

"And you never had more children?"

"We held things together a few more years. But Joanne's heart wasn't in it. I don't think life dealt her the cards she was expecting." He looked down at his plate then back at Marilyn. "She was a good enough person. She let me keep the house."

"That was kind of her."

"Well, it was mostly my money. But she could have been nasty about it." He took a sip of coffee. "Love's a strange kind of horse race, I guess."

Back on the porch, his thoughts were interrupted as Mike Rocket emerged from behind the house and went to his truck, returning with a clipboard. He stood in front of Carl on the sidewalk and made notes. "That's a big garage," he said. "Three cars' worth, I'll bet." He stopped as if counting something in his head then resumed. "The good news is that the floor's okay. And there's no rot or infestation. They built these places to last. The wiring will need help, but I know a guy who can keep the inspector off your back."

He turned the clipboard around and held it toward Carl, who regarded it warily. "Shouldn't someone else sign this?"

"I need your permission to start ripping up the house."

"Well, if that's all," Carl said. He signed by the X.

Mike tucked the clipboard under one arm. "All right, then, time to dance." He glanced through Carl's screen door. "You got a fridge and toilet in there, right?"

• • •

It took Carl almost a month to get used to the 5:30 rumble of Mike Rocket's power tools in the garage. With the renovation underway, he and Marilyn saw each other almost every day, though usually when she came to check on Mike's progress. It thrilled Carl to have her close, to feel her grab his arm or shoulder whenever she was admiring some new addition. Carl knew that he was tragically out of step with the world's idea of relationships. But patience had always been one of his defining qualities. He didn't mind waiting, and indeed everything he knew about the world suggested that to rush a thing was almost always to hasten it toward destruction.

Then came mid-May and Marilyn's biggest triumph for the show, when two Manhattan corporations agreed to loan the exhibit several Von Hersel pieces from their private collections. "They get a tax break," she told Carl and Mike. "It's a win-win situation." As she spoke, she kept one hand on Carl's forearm and the other around his waist, every now and then squeezing lightly. Carl was almost sad that the gesture made him happy. He felt sure there had been similar times with Joanne, but he could not remember one of them.

That night, after Mike had gone, Carl was not completely surprised when Marilyn took his arm and maneuvered him toward the stairs. If he'd worried about his sexual prowess—worried that there were things he'd forgotten or possibly never known—they were not an issue with Marilyn, who had no problem telling him what to do. Mainly she liked for him to lie on his back, perfectly still, his hands and feet pressed into the headboard and footboard, while she moved her hips around his in a rhythm that mixed circles and oblongs and straight lines in three dimensions. That first night he marveled at its intricacy, this woman's form tumbling around him like art—a great notion that could make him forget everything else, if only for a while.

When she had finished, Marilyn slid off of him and into the bed, falling asleep almost instantly. Carl waited a few minutes before rolling off the mattress, having learned as a young man that there was no use fighting his body when it didn't want to rest. He made his way downstairs to the kitchen and found a couple of Mike Rocket's seltzer waters lurking at the rear of the fridge, grabbed one by the neck, and twisted the cap into a satisfying hiss.

On the table, Marilyn had stacked an array of art books to cull for information for the tourists. With one finger, Carl flipped open the top volume to a page bookmarked with a strip of legal paper. There was a photo, a canvas completely covered with straight lines of various colors that crossed each other in an illusion of three dimensions, like a game of Pick-Up Sticks run amok. The caption read, *Georg Von Hersel (German-American, 1919–1967) explored the representational capacity of simple geometric patterns before turning to his better-known "straight line aesthetic," a provocative attempt to fuse the rational order of De Stijl with the subconscious impulses of abstract expressionism.*

For a second, Carl debated the TV in the other room then pulled another book from the pile. In a slightly longer biographical note, he learned that Von Hersel and his parents had fled from Austria to New York in 1933, presumably because of his mother's Jewish heritage. Von Hersel's father, a low-ranking civil servant, had pushed the younger Von Hersel toward a career in architecture and enrolled him at a technical school in Brooklyn. There, Georg Von Hersel developed a reputation for laziness with other subjects but repeatedly amazed his instructors when he drafted freehand more precisely than most of his peers could manage with a compass and straightedge.

After graduating, Von Hersel drifted between New York and

Boston, leaving or flunking out of the various colleges where he enrolled, sometimes for as little as a week. There was a falling out with his family, then a year and a half of complete silence before he ended up in Chicago in 1938, selling "geometric fancies" outside a local museum. Several museum patrons commissioned works—small fees for the most part, but enough to confirm Von Hersel's talent—and the rest was art history.

Carl leaned back in his chair to take a pull off the seltzer. He considered his kitchen wallpaper, salmon background with tiny, ivory fleur-de-lis at two-inch intervals. There were grease stains behind the oven, water marks near the ceiling, and several black abrasions that had been there when he bought the house. He wondered what Marilyn thought of his lack of decorating. He wondered why Joanne, in one of her fits of inspiration, had never chosen to repaint a room. After Von Hersel's departure for Chicago, the historical record did not mention his family again, despite his having two younger sisters in addition to his parents. Carl had a problem with that. When things had really started to go south with Joanne, he had done everything to help her: bought her supplies, driven her to shows, and left her alone to work when all he really wanted was someone to eat dinner with. He had never expected her to say thank-you or sorry. He really didn't want her to. But it bothered him that he'd never told her how, were it a girl, he had wanted to name their baby Elise, after his mother. Sitting at the table, he decided that he should have at least told her that.

Von Hersel himself had been briefly married, but his wife had died only three months after the ceremony, complications from scarlet fever. A footnote indicated how, years later, the artist had donated several paintings to a Virginia hospital for perfecting a surgical technique that would have kept his wife alive. But he never married again. He returned from Chicago to New York and tried to cultivate a reputation as a drinker, gambler, and womanizer. In reality, he was only the first: much and often.

There were colorful episodes. Von Hersel claimed once to have come to blows with Jackson Pollock after an all-night drinking bout and later sold the blood-stained white Oxford that he'd purportedly been wearing during the fight, having pinned it to a corkboard and entitled it "Pollock's Latest." Another time, he was hired by a Midtown gallery to give an exhibition of his technique and demanded a thirty-foot canvas for the occasion. After more than his share of champagne, and at the behest of the gallery director, he borrowed a tube of red lipstick from one of the waitresses, drew a single line the entire length of the canvas, then turned and walked out the front door. The audience of socialites was livid, and it was not until several days later that the director discovered what he claimed to have suspected all along: Von Hersel's lipstick was equidistant from the top and bottom of the canvas along its entire thirty-foot length. Even half-drunk, he had drawn a perfectly straight line.

So maybe, Carl figured, he was missing the point when he noted what a shambles the artist's life had been, big payoffs that led only to binges followed by three months in someone's garage. Von Hersel was clearly a genius as a painter, but as a man, he was no better than most and worse than many. Some of the books Carl read spent several pages trying to explain why Von Hersel had started to emphasize straight lines in his work, but Carl didn't need an explanation. An imperious father, a dead wife, a bottle for a confidante, and God knew what else—everything was blind curves, diversions, or dead ends. It was only in Von Hersel's art that lines were possible. Finality. Or, if he preferred, infinity—straightness like a tightrope, like an escape route, the only trick to find a canvas large enough to take in everything it needed to.

• • •

Three months after their first date, it vaguely occurred to Carl that Marilyn still had not told him much about herself. He knew that she came from money, that her parents had died when she was very young, and that she had spent the subsequent years living off their estate. He knew also that she had grown up in Manhattan and never worked a real job, dropping out of Barnard to take an unpaid internship at MOMA, which she quit when they stopped letting her walk around after hours. She had been in Hastings for two years, ever since the city became "Disneyland North," but refused to buy a house because she knew, sooner or later, that she would flee the provincialism of Westchester, too. When Carl showed her the loom in his basement, she referred to Joanne as a "crafts person" in a voice that could have frozen kerosene. And she never seemed to have an emotion wholly her own but insisted on describing her moods in terms of artists: calm Seurat, confused Dali, depressed Pollock, efficient Mondrian.

But for all that, Carl felt like she opened up to him as much as she did to anyone. She did not have other close friends or family, as near as he could tell, and when she told him that art intrigued her because it forced the artist to be unavoidably true and false at the same time, he wondered if she weren't saying something about herself. Another time, over Chinese food at her apartment, Carl caught her staring at him in a way that made him believe he was never meant to understand her. He'd been rehashing the takeout menu and paused between the Hunan Scallops and Lake Tung Ting Shrimp, when he looked up at her. "The problem," she said without provocation, "is that I've never made a choice. I want to care about people as much as I do about art. But I'm convinced that we each get only so much love in this world, and I'm using mine up."

The idea came back to Carl while he was clearing packing straps out of his driveway. Up ahead, he could see the brake lights of the red and black armored car as it pulled onto the street. Behind him, from the garage, he could hear Marilyn giving instructions as Mike Rocket wedged the crates open, the shrill complaint of nails pulled from wood echoing through the back yard.

With less than a week before the exhibit, they were almost done. Mike had leveled the garage floor, hung drywall, and even built a free-standing exhibit wall with track lighting in the garage's center. Two window-unit air conditioners pumped in a relaxing breeze, and Marilyn had erected a small table in a front corner of the garage on which she had piled various Society brochures. The mounted posters from the copy store had arrived a day earlier—an assortment of information about Von Hersel's life, critical analyses, and a history of art in the Hudson Valley. They had even installed an alarm system per the insurance company's guidelines, though, for liability purposes, Marilyn told them, only she was allowed to know the arming code.

"So how much are these things worth?" Carl could hear Mike saying.

"At last two million. Maybe three, depending on the market."

"Three million dollars? Jesus," Mike exclaimed, "you could buy a minor league ball club."

There were four canvases in all, none bigger than the top of a TV tray. Carl's favorite was a piece called *Blue Spectrum 6,* a series of six-inch blue lines like standing men beginning at the left of the canvas, curving a little past its middle, then descending to disappear at the canvas's bottom. Where they began and ended, the lines were so dark that they were barely distinguishable from the painted background, but as they made their way inward, they lightened to the point of turning almost white. It was only by great straining of his eyes that Carl could make out the slight cyan tint where the inmost lines reached their apogee. Marilyn held the canvas at eye level and made him look at it from the side. From the oblique angle, and at her prompting, he saw that what he originally assumed to be a black background was actually the darkest navy blue, blending with the darkest of the lines superimposed on it. Each line was of uniform thinness, and it was only at the curve in the canvas's middle, where angles forced the lines to separate, that one could see them at all. Otherwise it was a seamless movement, different colors that remained somehow the same.

When they had finished hanging the canvases, Marilyn went to her portfolio and returned with title placards for each piece as well as two smaller mounted posters that listed the corporate donors. She used a small digital camera to take pictures of the paintings by themselves, then with herself, Carl, and Mike standing beside them. At last they took a stroll around the perimeter of the garage, then Mike and Carl waited in the driveway as Marilyn set the alarm. Just as they reached the front porch, though, she lifted a hand to her shoulder and said, "My bag," then rolled her eyes in exasperation. "I'll be right back."

As she returned to the garage, Mike extended his hand to Carl. "Nice working with you, bud." He held Carl's hand tight for a second, then said, "You know, even righteous love's a kick in the teeth."

Carl did not respond. Mike went on to explain how he'd reached the conclusion a night earlier, while watching a sci-fi flick about the spider queen on late-night cable. The spider queen had black hair and eyes, eight arms constantly angling toward self-embrace, and a spandex-sequin bodysuit that covered only the most strategic areas. "You'd think," Mike concluded, "I'd know what I want in a woman by now."

"Knowing and finding are different things," Carl said. He suddenly realized that Marilyn had been gone longer than expected, some last-minute cleanup perhaps, and wondered if he should go help her.

Mike looked across the yard and into the trees, beyond which was the Hudson River, visible from the house only in winter. "You're one of the good guys, Carl," he chuckled. "Last of the breed." He swung into his truck, and they turned to see Marilyn emerging from the garage, bag draped over her shoulder. "I'll be on the cell if there are problems," he told them both before pulling out.

When the pickup had passed from view, Carl turned to Marilyn. "You're sure you won't stay for dinner?" He wasn't surprised when she shook her head. She had a meeting in Bronxville the next day, and it would be a much shorter drive from her place in Hastings. He tried a different tack. "You know, I have some vacation saved up. Maybe after the exhibit we could take a trip. You been to the Caribbean?"

For a second he could not tell if she had heard him. Her chin pulled slightly inward, as if she'd taken a bite of something more sour than she'd expected. "Carl," she said, "we shouldn't get our hopes up yet."

Carl held up both hands. "Oh, yeah. Listen, I'm not talking long-term. Just a break, is all."

"I'm not the beach type."

"Vermont, then. We'll have time to talk. Or not talk. Whatever."

She thought about it, then smiled a little. "Just let me get through Monday, okay?" She leaned forward to kiss him. "I'll call you tomorrow."

"It's a date," Carl said. He closed the car door after she'd slipped inside then waited until the Cadillac reached the end of the street before he waved and returned to the house.

• • •

She did not call the next day, a Friday. Carl wasn't worried—sometimes she got busy. But he grew concerned when he had not heard from her by the time he returned from work on Saturday. He called several times and, when that failed, drove to Hastings to let himself in. Everything seemed normal, leftovers in the fridge and a couple of telemarketers on the answering machine. He was just about to call the hospitals when a strange thought hit him. He went to her bedroom closet. No clothes.

The ride back to Cold Spring seemed to take twice as long as usual.

He missed every light on Route 9 and wound up behind a wide-load truck toting half of a modular home. By the time he reached the house, he'd lost all sense of caution. He unlocked the side door of the garage and turned the handle, expecting the alarm to go off. When nothing happened, he reached inside and fumbled with the light switches, then pulled his body fully through the door to confirm what he had feared. All of the paintings were gone, razor-cut off of their wooden frames. A few bits of canvas remained, stapled or glued to the sides of the wood. But in the frame's centers, only air and the too-bright glow of Mike Rocket's track lighting.

He took an hour to collect himself before contacting the police. When pressed, he told them only that he had grown concerned about Marilyn when she had not responded to any of his phone calls. He gave them the spare key to her apartment, but lied when they asked why he had it and said that he had visited her once and seen where she hid it in a flower pot. They came back over each of the next few days, always with questions, rifling through the garage and searching the house. He kept his answers simple. Three full days after the exhibit had been slated to begin, he realized no one had ever shown up. It was possible, certainly, that the Society had managed to cancel the Von Hersel tour stop in time. But more likely, he knew, there never had been a Von Hersel stop—a fact he confirmed a week later when he took some of Marilyn's brochures to the Society office and showed the lady at the front desk. "The police have already been here," she said, then showed him where Marilyn's event had been added to the Society's legitimate brochure. "They think she stole some of our graphics files," the woman continued. "It would have been easy to doctor the brochure from there."

Even Mike Rocket was startled at first. "Who would have guessed?" he said. Despite the situation, Carl felt strangely relieved to learn that the contractor had not been part of the scheme. "Look," Mike continued, "I don't want to kick you when you're down. I can use the air conditioners on another job. And I'll check the bill to see where I can cut you a break." He looked at the garage, then back at Carl. "I didn't tell the police everything about the two of you." He put his hand on Carl's shoulder and left it there a few seconds. "It could have happened to anybody."

But Carl wasn't so sure. By the next week, he'd hired a lawyer. He searched the yellow pages until he found one he could afford, a young Ossining guy who got carded with every beer he ordered during their "strategy" lunches. Carl endured a string of depositions and three court appearances in Manhattan, listening as the insurance company made him out to be a criminal genius. They sent investigators to his home, his workplace, his bank, and throughout town. They reviewed credit card receipts, check books, and phone records. For three months after the theft—with his lawyer's consent—they even got to open his mail. Eight months passed before a judge put a stop to things, noting that Carl's only crime was 'unfortunate, if complete, stupidity.' Afterward, Carl thanked his lawyer, who shrugged and said, "It's never really over, you know?"

The package showed up several months later—a padded manila mailer left by his back door, no return address. Inside were fifty thousand dollars in cash, a picture of Marilyn and Carl in front of *Blue Spectrum 6*, and a note that read: "When it mattered most, I meant everything I said. Take care of yourself. Marilyn."

Crazy as it was, he wanted to believe her. Shortly after the theft, it became clear that Marilyn had been careful not to leave behind any images of herself—for fear of being identified, the police said. Yet here Carl had a perfect picture with which to do what he pleased. He wanted to believe that she knew he would not turn it over, that he would keep it in the hope of their meeting again. The chance was faint, but he imagined it anyway. Somewhere in the Midwest, or Canada, or Europe, or on a Caribbean cruise, she would be there, letting herself into his room with a key that she possessed without his giving it to her. He almost believed that she loved him.

And then he realized that he did not even know if Marilyn were her real name.

The art books were still on his kitchen table. In the year that had passed, he had not bothered to move them but merely stacked them in one corner. He flipped one open to where several Von Hersel paintings shone up from the page, and he thought what a curse it was to be stupid or brilliant. Or anywhere in between, for that matter. Straight lines always found the edge of the canvas. Straight roads stopped at the horizon. But there must have been a place, Ashtabula maybe, where the straight lines went just far enough to reach the houses of lovers, sure in their desire for each other. He imagined them together, the two bodies made one body, a single line of flesh and meaning—then closed the book. Lines could get most people only so far, he figured. It was the places without geometry that were tough. He tossed Marilyn's note into the trash, then considered the photo before tucking it under his forearm with the money and heading to the back door. In the garage, he hid the money in the ceiling loft from which Mike Rocket had never bothered to remove the odd lumber pieces that had been there since Carl bought the house. He took the picture into the exhibit room and balanced it on one of the wooden frames that had supported the canvases, the one for *Blue Spectrum 6.* They were all still there, like empty eyes. Carl tried not to feel anything as he looked at them. He was getting tired. He killed the lights, set the alarm, and went back to the house.

The Death of the Short Story

The Story's death caught us all off guard. We'd been watching Poetry so closely that we failed to heed the warning signs. One day the Story was here, watching football, going to singles bars, making quiche. The next day—POOF!—we were reading about his demise in the *Times*, our bagels forgotten, our untouched lattes forming white rings on the dark wood of our kitchen tables.

Naturally there was a public outcry. On TV, we watched the crowds stack flowers and stuffed animals outside libraries worldwide. Soon the talk shows buzzed with innuendo. *A genre cut down in its prime,* they claimed. Audiences were stunned when the Memoir admitted to an affair with the Story during her "reconstructed memory" phase. Media scrutiny became so intense that the entire Autobiography family left town for a month to work out its issues in private.

At the funeral, the Prose Poem delivered a eulogy where she referred to publishers as "market whores" and called academics "literary vultures happier since the Story's departure." But in truth, we were all to blame. We milled around the reception feeling sheepish, thinking about what we might have done. In a corner, the loutish Novel got drunk on cheap Chardonnay and babbled about the good times he and the Story had shared. He consoled himself by hugging random passers-by and saying "I Love You!" much too loudly for the comfort of the lit-mag editors several feet away.

In the weeks that followed, rumors began to circulate about how the Story's brain had been cryogenically stored in a bunker near Omaha. A Glasgow professor offered a thousand pounds to anyone who could produce a sample of the Story's DNA, for cloning purposes. Still others maintained that the Story was not gone at all, but had faked his death and retired to an isolated mountain retreat in the Andes or the Himalayas.

This last idea redeemed us somehow. We began to make up lies about the Story, lies which seemed like truth after a while. We pictured the Story sitting around a fireplace with John Lennon, Jesus, and Amelia Earhart, where they sipped century-old cognac and talked about what players to put on their All-Time Fantasy Baseball Teams. They wore the socks that we'd lost in the dryer over the years and jangled the spare change that had dropped between our sofa cushions. A single bay window looked out over the mountains from which they could see, above the clouds, a spinning whirlpool of various colors. The colors, they imagined, were their dreams, and they waited patiently for those moments when a sliver of light would break loose from the oblong, suspended momentarily like a musical note on fire before streaking recklessly into the surrounding night.